A
GRANDMOTHER'S
RECOLLECTIONS

ELLA RODMAN

A Grandmother's Recollections

Ella Rodman

© 1st World Library, 2009
PO Box 2211
Fairfield, IA 52556
www.1stworldlibrary.com
First Edition

LCCN: 2009923409

Softcover ISBN: 978-1-4218-8829-3
Hardcover ISBN: 978-1-4218-8928-3
eBook ISBN: 978-1-4218-8730-2

Purchase *"A Grandmother's Recollections"*
as a traditional bound book at:
www.1stWorldLibrary.com/purchase.asp?ISBN=978-1-4218-8829-3

1st World Library is a literary, educational organization
dedicated to:

- Creating a free internet library of downloadable ebooks

- Hosting writing competitions and offering book publishing
  scholarships.

1st World Library Literary Society

Giving Back to the World

"If you want to work on the core problem, it's early school literacy."

- James Barksdale, former CEO of Netscape

"No skill is more crucial to the future of a child, or to a democratic and prosperous society, than literacy."

- Los Angeles Times

"Literacy... means far more than learning how to read and write... The aim is to transmit... knowledge and promote social participation."

- UNESCO

"Literacy is not a luxury, it is a right and a responsibility. If our world is to meet the challenges of the twenty-first century we must harness the energy and creativity of all our citizens."

- President Bill Clinton

"Parents should be encouraged to read to their children, and teachers should be equipped with all available techniques for teaching literacy, so the varying needs and capacities of individual kids can be taken into account."

- Hugh Mackay

CHAPTER I

The best bed-chamber, with its hangings of crimson moreen, was opened and aired—a performance which always caused my eight little brothers and sisters to place themselves in convenient positions for being stumbled over, to the great annoyance of industrious damsels, who, armed with broom and duster, endeavored to render their reign as arbitrary as it was short. For some time past, the nursery-maids had invariably silenced refractory children with "Fie, Miss Matilda! Your grandmother will make you behave yourself —*she* won't allow such doings, I'll be bound!" or "Aren't you ashamed of yourself, Master Clarence? What will your grandmother say to that!" The nursery was in a state of uproar on the day of my venerable relative's arrival; for the children almost expected to see, in their grandmother, an ogress, both in features and disposition.

My mother was the eldest of two children, and my grand-mother, from the period of my infancy, had resided in England with her youngest daughter; and we were now all employed in wondering what sort of a person our relative might be. Mamma informed us that the old lady was extremely dignified, and exacted respect and attention from all around; she also hinted, at the same time, that it would be well for me to lay aside a little of my self-sufficiency, and accommodate myself to the humors of my grandmother. This to me!—to *me*, whose temper was so inflammable that the least inadvertent touch was sufficient to set it in a blaze—it was too much! So, like a well-disposed young lady, I very properly resolved that *mine* should not be the arm to support the venerable Mrs. Arlington in her daily walks; that should the children playfully ornament the cushion of her easy-chair with pins, *I* would not turn informant; and should a conspiracy be on foot to burn the old lady's best wig, I entertained serious thoughts of helping along myself.

In the meantime, like all selfish persons, I considered what demeanor I should assume, in order to impress my grandmother with a conviction of my own consequence. Of course, dignified and unbending I *would* be; but what if she chose to consider me a child, and treat me accordingly? The idea was agonizing to my feelings; but then I proudly surveyed my five feet two inches of height, and wondered how I could have thought of such a thing! Still I had sense enough to know that such a supposition would never have entered my head, had there not been sufficient grounds for it; and, with no small trepidation, I prepared for my first appearance.

It went off as first appearances generally do. I *was* to have been seated in an attitude of great elegance, with my eyes fixed on the pages of some wonderfully wise book, but my thoughts anywhere but in company with my eyes; while, to give more dignity to a girlish figure, my hair was to be turned up on the very top of my head with a huge shell comb, borrowed for the occasion from mamma's drawer. Upon my grandmother's entrance, I intended to rise and make her a very stiff courtesy, and then deliver a series of womanish remarks. This, I say, *was* to have been my first appearance—but alas! fate ordered otherwise. I was caught by my dignified relative indulging in a game of romps upon the balcony with two or three little sisters in pinafores and pantalettes—myself as much a child as any of them. My grandmother came rather suddenly upon me as, with my long hair floating in wild confusion, I stooped to pick up my comb; and while in this ungraceful position, one of the little urchins playfully climbed upon my back, while the others held me down. My three little sisters had never appeared to such disadvantage in my eyes, as they did at the present moment; in vain I tried to shake them off—they only clung the closer, from fright, on being told of their grandmother's arrival.

At length, with crimsoned cheeks, and the hot tears starting to my eyes, I rose and received, rather than returned the offered embrace, and found myself in the capacious arms of one whom I should have taken for an old dowager duchess. On glancing at my grandmother's portly figure and cones-quential air, I experienced the uncomfortable sensation of utter insignificance—I encountered the gaze of those full, piercing eyes, and felt that I was conquered. Still I resolved to make some struggles for my dignity yet, and not submit until defeat was no longer doubtful. People in talking of "unrequited affection," speak of "the knell of departed hopes," but no knell could sound more dreadful to the ears of a girl in her teens—trembling for her scarcely-fledged young-lady-hood—than did the voice of my grandmother, (and it was by no means low), as she remarked:

"So this is Ella. Why, how the child has altered! I remember her only as a little, screaming baby, that was forever holding its breath with passion till it became black in the face. Many a thumping have I given you, child, to make you come to, and sometimes I doubted if your face ever would be straight again. Even now it can hardly be said to belong to the meek and amiable order."

Here my grandmother drew forth her gold spectacles from a richly-ornamented case, and deliberately scanned my indign-ant features, while she observed: "Not much of the Bredforth style—quite an Arlington." I drew myself up with all the offended dignity of sixteen, but it was of no use; my grandmother turned me round, in much the same manner that the giant might have been supposed to handle Tom Thumb, and surveyed me from top to toe.

I was unable to discover the effect of her investigation, but I immediately became convinced that my grandmother's opinion was one of the greatest importance. She possessed that indescribable kind of manner which places you under the conviction that you are continually doing, saying, or thinking something wrong; and which makes you humbly obliged to such a person for coinciding in any of your opinions. Instead of the dignified part I had expected to play, I looked very like a naughty child that has just been taken out of its corner. The impression left upon my mind by my grandmother's appearance will never be effaced; her whole *tout ensemble* was peculiarly striking, with full dark eyes, high Roman nose, mouth of great beauty and firmness of expression, and teeth whose splendor I have never seen equalled—although she was then past her fiftieth year. Add to this a tall, well-proportioned figure, and a certain air of authority, and my grandmother stands before you.

As time somewhat diminished our awe, we gained the *entree* of my grandmother's apartment, and even ventured to express our curiosity respecting the contents of various trunks, parcels, and curious-looking boxes. To children, there is no greater pleasure than being permitted to look over and arrange the articles contained in certain carefully-locked up drawers, unopened boxes, and old-fashioned chests; stray jewels from broken rings—two or three beads of a necklace —a sleeve or breadth of somebody's wedding dress—locks of hair—gifts of schoolgirl friendships—and all those little mementoes of the past, that lie neglected and forgotten till a search after some mislaid article brings them again to our view, and excites a burst of feeling that causes us to look sadly back upon the long vista of departed years, with their withered hopes, never-realized expectations, and fresh, joyous tone, seared by disappointment and worldly wisdom. The reward of patient toil and deep-laid schemes yields not half the pleasure that did the little Indian cabinet, (which always stood so provokingly locked, and just within reach), when during a period of convalescence, we were permitted to examine its recesses—when floods of sunlight danced upon the wall of the darkened room towards the close of day, and every one seemed *so* kind!

My grandmother indulged our curiosity to the utmost; now a pair of diamond ear-pendants would appear among the soft folds of perfumed cotton, and flash and glow with all the brilliancy of former days—now a rich brocaded petticoat called up phantoms of the past, when ladies wore high-heeled shoes, and waists of no size at all—and gentlemen felt magnificently attired in powdered curls and cues, and as many ruffles as would fill a modern dressing gown. There were also fairy slippers, curiously embroidered, with neatly covered heels; and anxious to adorn myself with these relics of the olden time I attempted to draw one on. But like the renowned glass-slipper, it would fit none but the owner, and I found myself in the same predicament as Cinderella's sisters. In vain I tugged and pulled; the more I tried, the more it wouldn't go on—and my grandmother remarked with a sigh, that "people's feet were not as small as they were in old times." I panted with vexation; for I had always been proud of my foot, and now put it forward that my grandmother might see how small it was. But no well-timed compliment soothed my irritated feelings; and more dissatisfied with myself than ever, I pursued my investigations.

My grandmother, as if talking to herself, murmured: "How little do we know, when we set out in life, of the many dis-appointments before us! How little can we deem that the heart which then is ours will change with the fleeting sun-shine! It is fearful to have the love of a life-time thrown back as a worthless thing!"

"Fearful!" I chimed in. "Death were preferable!"

"You little goose!" exclaimed my grandmother, as she looked me full in the face, "What can *you* possibly know about the matter?"

I had nothing to do but bury my head down low in the trunk I was exploring; it was my last attempt at sentiment. My grandmother took occasion to give me some very good advice with respect to the behavior of hardly-grown girls; she remarked that they should be careful not to engross the conversation, and also, that quiet people were always more interesting than loud talkers. I resolved to try my utmost to be quiet and interesting, though at the same time it did occur to me as a little strange that, being so great an admirer of the species, she was not quiet and interesting herself. But being quiet was not my grandmother's forte; and it is generally understood that people always admire what they are not, or have not themselves.

Ella Rodman

CHAPTER II

The old lady also possessed rather strict ideas of the respect and deference due to parents and elders; and poor mamma, whose authority did not stand very high, felt considerable relief in consequence of our, (or, as I am tempted to say, *the children's*) improved behavior. I remember being rather startled myself one day, when one of the before-mentioned little sisters commenced a system of teazing for some forbidden article.

"Mother, mother,—can't I have that set of cards? We want it in our play-room—Phemie and me are going to build a house."

"I do not like to give you permission," replied mamma, looking considerably worried, "for George does not wish you to have them."

"Oh, but George is out, mother—out for all day," rejoined the precocious canvasser, "and will never know anything about it."

"But perhaps he might come home before you had done with them, and George is so terribly passionate, and hates to have his things touched, that he will raise the whole house."

"Poor boy!" observed my grandmother dryly, "What a

misfortune to be so passionate! A deep-seated, and, I fear, incurable one, Amy; for of course you have used your utmost endeavors, both by precept and example, to render him otherwise."

I almost pitied my mother's feelings; for well did I remember the cried-for toy placed within his hands, to stop the constant succession of screams sent forth by a pair of lungs whose strength seemed inexhaustible—the comfort and convenience of the whole family disregarded, not because he was the *best*, but the *worst* child—and often the destruction of some highly-prized trinket or gem of art, because he was "*passionate*;" the result of which was, that my poor brother George became one of the most selfish, exacting, intolerable boys that ever lived.

There was no reply, save a troubled look; and the little tormentor continued in a fretful tone; "We'll put 'em all away before he gets in, and never tell him a word of it—can't we have them, mother?"

My mother glanced towards her mentor, but the look which she met impelled her to pursue a course so different from her usual one, that I listened in surprise: "No, Caroline, you can *not* have them—now leave the room, and let me hear no more about it."

"I want them," said the child in a sullen tone, while she turned to that invariable resource of refactory children who happen to be near a door; namely, turning the knob, and clicking the lock back and forth, and swinging on it at intervals.

This performance is extremely trying to a person of restless, nervous temperament, and my grandmother, setting up her spectacles, exclaimed commandingly: "Caroline, how dare you stand pouting there? Did you not hear your mother, naughty girl? Leave the room—this instant?"

The child stood a moment almost transfixed with surprise; but as she saw my grandmother preparing to advance upon her—her ample skirts and portly person somewhat resembling a ship under full sail—she made rather an abrupt retreat; discomposing the nerves of a small nursery-maid, whom she encountered in the passage, to such a degree that, as the girl expressed it, "she was took all of a sudden."

I had given a quick, convulsive start as the first tones fell upon my ear, and now sat bending over my sewing like a chidden child, almost afraid to look up. I was one of those unlucky mortals who bear the blame of everything wrong they witness; and having, in tender infancy, been suddenly seized upon in Sunday school by the superintendent, and placed in a conspicuous situation of disgrace for looking at a companion who was performing some strange antic, but who possessed one of those india-rubber faces that, after twisting themselves into all possible, or rather impossible shapes, immediately become straight the moment any one observes them—having, I say, met with this mortifying exposure, it gave me a shock which I have not to this day recovered; and I cannot now see any one start up hastily in pursuit of another without fancying myself the culprit, and trembling accordingly. This sudden movement, therefore, of my grandmother's threw me into an alarming state of terror, and, quite still and subdued, I sat industriously stitching, all the morning after.

"Dear me!" said my mother with a sigh, "how much better you make them mind than I can."

"I see, Amy," said my grandmother kindly, "that your influence is very weak—the care of of so large a family has prevented you from attending to each one properly. You perceive the effect of a little well-timed authority, and I do not despair of you yet. You are naturally," she continued, "amiable and indolent, and though gentleness is certainly agreeable and interesting, yet a constant succession of sweets cannot fail to cloy, and engender a taste for something sharper and more wholesome."

Delicacy prevented me from remaining to hear my mother advised and lectured, and the rest of my grandmother's discourse was therefore lost to me; but whatever it was, I soon perceived its beneficial results—the children were no longer permitted to roam indiscriminately through all parts of the house—certain rooms were proof againt their invasions—they became less troublesome and exacting, and far more companionable. The worried look gradually cleared from my mother's brow, and as my grandmother was extremely fond of sight-seeing, visiting, tea-drinkings, and everything in the shape of company, she persevered in dragging her daughter out day after day, until she made her enjoy it almost as much as herself. Old acquaintances were hunted up and brought to light, and new ones made through the exertions of my grandmother, who, in consequence of such a sociable disposition, soon became very popular. The young ones were banished to the nursery; and, as they were no longer allowed to spend their days in eating, there was far less sickness among them, and our family doctor's bill decreased amazingly.

Our grandmother, having spent many years in the "mother-country," was extremely English in her feelings and opinions, and highly advocated the frugal diet on which the children of the higher classes are always kept. Lord and Lady Grantham, the son-in-law and daughter at whose residence she passed the time of her sojourn in England, were infallible models of excellence and prudence; and the children were again and again informed that their little English cousins were never allowed meat until the age of seven, and considered it a great treat to get beef broth twice a week. Butter was also a prohibited article of luxury—their usual breakfast consisting of mashed potatoes, or bread and milk;

Ella Rodman

and my grandmother used to relate how one morning a little curly-headed thing approached her with an air of great mystery, and whispered: "What *do* you think we had for breakfast?" "Something very good, I suspect—what can it be?" "Guess." "O, I cannot; you must tell me." "*Buttered bread*!" Our laughter increased as she gave an amusing account of the blue eyes stretched to their utmost extent, as these wonderful words were pronounced hesitatingly, as though doubtful of the effect; and in consequence of various anecdotes of the same nature, the children's impressions of England were by no means agreeable. Our little cousins must certainly have been the most wonderful children ever heard of, for by my grandmother's account, they could dance, sing, and speak French almost as soon as they could walk. She also informed us, as a positive fact, that on saying: "*Baisez, Cora—baisez la dame*," the very baby in arms put up its rosebud lips to kiss the stranger mentioned. It would have been stranger still for the younger children to speak English, as they were always in the company of French nurses.

Although my grandmother could so easily assume a stern and commanding air, it was by no means habitual to her; and the children, though they feared and never dared to dispute her authority, soon loved her with all the pure, unselfish love of childhood, which cannot be bought. "Things were not so and so when I was young," was a favorite remark of hers; and as I one day remarked that "those must have been wonderful times when old people were young," she smiled and said that "though not wonderful, they were times when parents and teachers were much more strict with children than they are now." I immediately experienced a strong desire to be made acquainted with the circumstances of my grandmother's childhood, and began hinting to that effect.

"Were they very strict with you, grandmother?" asked we mischievously.

She looked rather disconcerted for a moment, and then replied with a smile: "Not very—I saw very little of my parents, being mostly left to nurses and servants; but you all seem eager for information on that point, and although there is absolutely nothing worth relating, you may all come to my room this evening, and we will begin on the subject of my younger days."

We swallowed tea rather hastily, and danced off in high glee to my grandmother's apartment, ready for the unfolding of unheard-of occurrences and mysteries.

Ella Rodman

CHAPTER III

We were all happily seated around the fire; the grate was piled up high with coal, and threw a bright reflection upon the polished marble—everything was ready to begin, when a most unfortunate question of my sister Emma's interfered with our progress. She had settled herself on a low stool at my grandmother's feet, and while we all sat in silent expectation of the "once upon a time," or "when I was young," which is generally the prelude to similar narratives, Emma suddenly started up, and fixing an incredulous gaze upon our dignified relative, exclaimed: "But were you *ever* young, grandmother? I mean," she continued, a little frightened at her own temerity, "were you ever as little as I am now?"

Some of us began to cough, others used their pocket-hand-kerchiefs, and one and all waited in some anxiety for the effect. Emma, poor child! seemed almost ready to sink through the floor under the many astonished and reproving glances which she encountered; and my grandmother's countenance at first betokened a gathering storm.

But in a few moments this cleared up; and ashamed of her momentary anger at this childish question, she placed her hand kindly on Emma's head as she replied: "Yes, Emma, quite as little as you are—and it is of those very times that I am going to tell you. I shall not begin at the beginning, but speak of whatever happens to enter my mind, and a complete history of my childhood will probably furnish employment for a great many evenings. But I am very much averse to interruptions, and if you have any particular questions to ask, all inquiries must be made before I commence."

"Were you born and did you live in America?" said I.

"Yes," replied my grandmother, "I was born and lived in America, in the State of New York. So much for the locality —now, what next?"

"Did you ever see Washington?" inquired Bob, "And were you ever taken prisoner and had your house burned by the British?"

Bob was a great patriot, and on Saturdays practised shooting in the attic with a bow and arrow, to perfect himself against the time of his attaining to man's estate, when he fully intended to collect an army and make an invasion on England. As an earnest of his hostile intentions, he had already broken all the windows on that floor, and nearly extinguished the eye of Betty, the chambermaid. To both of these questions my grandmother replied in the negative, for she happened to come into the world just after the Revolution; but in answer to Bob's look of disappointment, she promised to tell him something about it in the course of her narrative.

"My two most prominent faults," said she, "were vanity and curiosity, and these both led me into a great many scrapes, which I shall endeavor to relate for your edification. I shall represent them just as they really were, and if I do not make especial comments on each separate piece of misconduct, it is because I leave you to judge for yourselves, by placing them in their true light. I shall not tell you the year I was born in," she continued, "for then there would be a counting on certain little fingers to see how old grandmamma is now. When I was a child—a *very* young one—I used to say that I

Ella Rodman

remembered very well the day on which I was born, for mother was down stairs frying dough-nuts. This nondescript kind of cake was then much more fashionable for the tea-table than it is at the present day. My mother was quite famous for her skill in manufacturing them, and my great delight was to superintend her operations, and be rewarded for good behavior with a limited quantity of dough, which I manufactured into certain uncouth images, called 'dough-nut babies.' Sometimes these beloved creations of genius performed rather curious gymnastics on being placed in the boiling grease—such as twisting on one side, throwing a limb entirely over their heads, &c.; while not unfrequently a leg or an arm was found missing when boiled to the requisite degree of hardness. But sometimes, oh, sad to relate! my fingers committed such unheard-of depredations in the large bowl or tray appropriated by my mother, that I was sentenced to be tied in a high chair drawn close to her side, whence I could quietly watch her proceedings without being able to assist her.

I know that our home was situated in a pleasant village which has long since disappeared in the flourishing city; the house was of white brick, three stories high, with rooms on each side of the front entrance. A large and beautiful flower-garden was visible from the back windows; and beyond this was a still larger fruit-garden, the gate of which was generally locked, while a formidable row of nails with the points up, repelled all attempts at climbing over the fence. The peaches, and plums, apricots, nectarines, grapes, cherries, and apples were such as I have seldom, if ever, seen since. My lather was wealthy, and my earliest recollections are connected with large, handsomely-furnished rooms, numerous servants, massive plate, and a constant succession of dinner-parties and visitors. How often have I watched the servants as they filled the decanters, rubbed the silver, and made other preparations for company, while I drew comparisons between the lot of the favored beings for whom these preparations were made, and my own, on being condemned to the unvarying routine of the nursery. Childhood then appeared to me a kind of penance which we were doomed to undergo—a sort of imprisonment or chrysalis, which, like the butterfly, left us in a fairy-like and beautiful existence. Little did I then dream of the cares, and toils, and troubles from which that happy season is exempt. My father realized in his own person, to the fullest extent, all the traditionary legends of old English hospitality; he hated everything like parsimony—delighted to see his table surrounded with visitors—and in this was indulged to the extent of his wishes; for day after day seemed to pass in our being put out of sight, where we could witness the preparations going on for other people's entertainment.

The presiding goddess in our region of the house was a faithful and attached old nurse, whom we all called 'Mammy.' Although sometimes a little sharp, as was necessary to keep such wild spirits in order, the old nurse was invariably kind, and even indulgent. It was well indeed for us that she was so, for we were left almost entirely to her direction, and saw very little of any one else. Mammy's everyday attire consisted of a calico short-gown, with large figures, and a stuff petticoat, with a cap whose huge ruffles stood up in all directions; made after a pattern which I have never since beheld, and in which the crown formed the principal feature. But this economical dress was not for want of means; for Mammy's wardrobe boasted several silk gowns, and visitors seldom stayed at the house without making her a present. On great occasions, she approached our beau-ideal of an empress, by appearing in a black silk dress lace collar, and gold repeater at her side. This particular dress Mammy valued more highly than any of the others, for my father had brought it to her, as a present, from Italy, and the pleasant consciousness of being recollected in this manner by her master was highly gratifying to the old nurse.

Ella Rodman

I was an only daughter, with several wild brothers, and I often thought that Mammy displayed most unjust partiality. For instance, there was Fred who never did anything right—upset his breakfast, dinner, and tea—several times set the clothes-horse, containing the nursery wardrobe, in a blaze—was forever getting lost, and, when sought for, often found dangling from a three-story window, hanging on by two fingers, and even one—who would scarcely have weighed a person's life in the scale with a successful joke—and always had a finger, foot, or eye bound up as the result of his hair-brained adventures. I really believe that Mammy bestowed all a mother's affection on this wild, reckless boy; he seldom missed an opportunity of being impertinent, and yet Mammy invariably said that 'Fred had a saucy tongue, but a good heart.' This *good-heartedness* probably consisted in drowning kittens, worrying dogs, and throwing stones at every bird he saw. Fred always had the warmest seat, the most thickly-buttered bread and the largest piece of pie. I remember one day on watching Mammy cut the pie, I observed, as usual, that she reserved the largest piece.

"Who is that for?" I enquired, although perfectly aware of its intended destination.

"O, no one in particular," replied Mammy.

"Well then" said I, "I believe I'll take it."

"There! there!" exclaimed Mammy, pointing her finger at me, "See the greedy girl! Now you shall not have it, just for asking for it." The disputed piece was immediately deposited on Fred's plate; and from that day forth I gave up all hopes of the largest piece of pie.

O, that Fred was an imp! There was nothing in the shape of mischief, which he would not do. If left to amuse the baby, he often amused himself by tying a string to its toe, and every now and then giving it a sudden pull. The child would cry, of course, and, on the approach of any one, Master Fred sat looking as demure as possible, while trying to keep his little brother quiet. The string would then be twitched again for his own private edification; and it was sometime before the trick was discovered. My brother Henry had at one time several little chickens, of which he became very fond. Day after day he fed, admired, and caressed them; and Fred, who never could bear to see others happy long, began to revolve in his own mind certain plans respecting the chickens. One by one they disappeared, until the number decreased alarmingly; but no traces of them could be found. We were questioned, but, as all denied the charge, the culprit remained undiscovered, although strong suspicions rested on Fred. At last the indignant owner came upon him one day, as he stood quietly watching the struggles of two little chickens in a tub of water. Henry bitterly exclaimed against this cruelty, but Fred innocently replied that "he had no hand in the matter; he had thought, for some time, how much prettier they would look swimming like ducks, and therefore tried to teach them—but the foolish things persisted in walking along with their eyes shut, and so got drowned."

But one of Fred's grand *coup-d'oeils* was the affair of the cherry-pie. In those days ladies attended more to their household affairs than they do at present; and my mother, an excellent housekeeper, was celebrated for her pastry— cherry-pies in particular. It was the Fourth of July; the boys were released from school, and roaming about in quest of mischief as boys always are—and, as a rare thing, we had no company that day, except my aunt, who had come from a distance on a visit to my mother, while my father had gone to return one of the numerous visits paid him. Cherry-pie was a standing dish at our house with which to celebrate the Declaration of Independence. The servants had all gone out for a holiday, no dinner was cooked, and the sole dependence was on the cherry-pie.

They sat down to dinner, and I heard my mother say: "Now, sister Berthy, I really hope you will enjoy this pie, for I bestowed extra pains upon it, and placed it up in the bed-room pantry out of the boys' reach, who are very apt to nibble off the edge of the crust. This time, I see, they have not meddled with it."

The pie was cut; but alas! for the hollowness of human triumphs; the knife met a wilderness of crust and vacancy, but no cherries. The bed-room pantry had a window opening on a shed, and into that window Fred, the scape-grace, had adroitly climbed, carefully lifted the upper crust from the cherished pie, and abstracted all the cherries. My mother locked him up, for punishment, but having unfortunately selected a sort of store-room pantry, he made himself sick with sweetmeats, broke all the jars he could lay hands on, and, finally, discovering a pair of scissors, he worked at the lock, spoiled it, and let himself out.

At one time, being rather short of cash, he helped himself to a five-dollar bill from my mother's drawer; but even *his* conscience scarcely resting under so heavy an embezzle-ment, he got it changed, took half a dollar, and then put the rest back in the drawer. This considerateness led to a discovery; they all knew that no one but Fred would have been guilty of so foolish, and at the same time so dishonest a thing.

My favorite brother was Henry; just three years older than myself, manly, amiable, and intellectual in his tastes, he appeared to me infinitely superior to any one I had ever seen; and we two were almost inseparable. In winter he always carried me to school on his sled, saw that Fred did not rob me of my dinner, and was always ready to explain a difficult lesson. He was an extremely enterprising boy, with an inexhaustible fund of ingenuity and invention; but, like most geniuses, received more blame than praise. When quite small he constructed a sort of gun made of wood, which would discharge a small ball of paper, pebble, &c. This became a very popular plaything in the nursery, and for once the inventor received due praise, on account of its keeping the children so quiet. But one day Fred undertook to teach the year old baby the art of shooting with it; and with a small corn for a bullet, he placed the toy in the child's hands, turning the mouth the wrong way. The young soldier pulled the trigger in delight, and by some strange mischance, the corn flew up his nose. The doctor was hastily brought, the child relieved with a great deal of difficulty, the dangerous plaything burned, and poor Henry sent to coventry for an unlimited time.

Ella Rodman

CHAPTER IV

We had a girl named Jane Davis whom my mother had brought up from childhood. At the period to which I refer, she could not have been more than fourteen, and as she was always good-humored and willing to oblige, she became a general favorite. Often, in the early winter evenings, with the nursery as tidy as hands could make it, (for Mammy, although not an old maid, was a mortal enemy to dirt and slovenliness) we all gathered round the fire, while the old nurse and Jane spun out long stories, sometimes of things which had happened to them, sometimes of things which had happened to others, and often of things that never did or could happen to anybody. But I must do them the justice to say, that although they sometimes related almost impossible occurrencies, they never, on any one occasion, took advantage of their influence over us to enforce our obedience by frighful tales of old men with bags, who seem to have an especial fancy for naughty children. The nearest approach that Mammy ever made to anything of this kind was to tell us, when we began to look sleepy, that the sandman had been along and filled our eyes. On receiving this information, we generally retired peaceably to bed, without being haunted by any fears of ghost or goblin.

There was a wealthy and fashionable family who lived just opposite, consisting of a widower, his sister, and two children—a son and daughter. They lived in most extravagant style, and Jane positively assured us that the housekeeper had told her with her own lips that there was no end to Mr. Okeman's wealth, and that he even made his daughter eat bank-bills on her bread and butter! Whether the son was exempted from this disagreeable performance we never thought of inquiring; but our awe rose ten percent, for a girl who was so rich as absolutely to devour money. On being divulged, this grand secret amused the inmates of the drawing-room very much, and our parents could scarcely command their countenances to undeceive us.

Jane Davis remained with us as nursery-maid until she was eighteen, when my mother, who was always extremely kind to servants and dependants, placed her at a trade, and supported her comfortably until she learned enough to support herself. She afterwards married a carpenter, who always performed for my father those odd jobs that are constantly required in a house, and they came to live in a kind of cottage at the end of the garden. They there commenced farming on a small scale, and often supplied us with milk, eggs, poultry, &c.

Mammy was a firm believer in signs of good and evil import; thus, if, in dropping the scissors, they stood up erect on the point, she always said that visitors were coming—a sign that rarely failed, as we were seldom a day without them. Once I had wished very much for a large wax-doll. My dreams were beautified with waxen images of immense size, whose china blue eyes, long flaxen curls, and rosy cheeks, presented a combination of charms that took my heart by storm. I sat one night, as usual, by the nursery fire; my thoughts fixed on this all-engrossing subject, when I ventured to communicate them to Mammy, and ask her if she thought I ever would become the enviable possessor of such a doll.

"I don't know," replied Mammy at first, "I think it's very

doubtful. But come here," she added, "and let me see your hand."

After an examination, Mammy pronounced with an air of great mystery that circumstances were propitious, and she was almost convinced beyond a doubt that ere long the doll would be mine. She then pointed out to me a small white spot on my left thumb nail, which she said always denoted a present. I was rather incredulous at first, not conceiving that so brilliant a dream could be realized; but after a while the doll actually made its appearance, and I began to regard Mammy as something little short of a witch, and became far more tractable in consequence of my increased awe.

Jane's stories, as well as Mammy's always began with "Once upon a time there were two sisters;" one was represented as plain-looking, but amiable—the other beautiful, but a very Zantippe in temper. By some wonderful combination of circumstances, the elder lost her beauty and ugliness at the same time—when some good fairy always came along, who, by a magic touch of her wand, made both the sisters far more lovely than the elder had been. Beauty was always the burden of the tale; people who were not beautiful met with no adventures, and seemed to lead a hum-drum sort of life; therefore, I insensibly learned to regard this wonderful possession as something very much to be desired. I believe I was quite a pretty child, with dark bright eyes, red lips, and a pair of very rosy cheeks. I spent considerable time before the glass, and both Mammy and Jane began to fear the effects of vanity. Often and often would the old nurse say: "You needn't stand before the glass, Miss Amy—there is nothing to look at," or when in a bad humor, "Don't make such faces, child—you have no beauty to spare," and I can very well remember how both would endeavor to persuade me that I was the most veritable little fright that ever existed, and quite a bugbear to my relations.

"What a pity," Jane would commence, as she saw me surveying myself with an air of infinite satisfaction, "what a pity it is that Miss Amy has such a dark, ugly skin—almost like an Indian, isn't it, nurse?"

I had eyes to judge for myself, and knew that I was much fairer than either Mammy or Jane; and somebody had re-marked in my presence: "What a lovely neck and shoulders!" therefore I generally remained perfectly quiet while listening to these inuendoes.

"Yes," Mammy would reply, "a very great pity—but an amiable temper, Miss Amy, is more than looks; you must try and cultivate that, to make up for your want of beauty."

"And then," continued Jane, "only see how perfectly straight her hair is! not a sign of curl, nor even a twist!—and black eyes have such a wicked kind of a look; they always remind me of cannibals."

Jane's eyes were as blue and bright as glass beads, while Mammy's, I thought, approached a green, but with my own I felt perfectly satisfied; for a lady had remarked in my presence what beautiful eyes I had—adding that "dark eyes were so much more expressive than blue; blue ones were so very insipid looking." The observation about my hair, though, was only too correct, and touched me most sensibly. While most of the other children possessed those soft, flowing curls, so beautiful in childhood, mine obstinately refused to wave; and was, to use Jane's expression, "as straight and as stiff as a poker." I had endeavored to remedy this as far as lay in my power, and one day set my hair in a blaze, while curling it with a very hot pipe-stem. I was, in consequence, deemed one of the most abandoned of the nursery inmates; and found myself minus at least one half of the hair I had hitherto possessed.

Ella Rodman

I really believe that both Jane and Mammy sincerely hoped to eradicate my besetting sin, by such blunt remarks as the former; but no course could have been less wise than the one which they took. I knew very well that I was neither a fright, an Indian, nor a cannibal; and the pains which they took to convince me to the contrary led me to give myself credit for much more beauty than I really possessed. I also regarded amiability as a virtue of very small account; and supposed that those who practised it, only did so because they possessed neither beauty, grace, nor anything else to recommend them.

A great source of annoyance to me was my dress. As I was an only daughter, some mothers, with the same means, would have enhanced my attractions with all the aid of ornament, and established me as a permanent divinity of the drawing-room, whom all must bow to and flatter as they entered its precincts. But, although fond of display, and surrounded with all the appliances of wealth, the taste of my parents never did run much on dress; and I often felt mortified at my inferiority to others in this respect. Such articles were then much dearer, and more in vogue than at the present day, and a blue Circassian formed my entire stock of gala dresses, and went the rounds of all the children's parties I attended; my mother seemed to think, (with respect to me, at least,) that as long as a dress was clean and in good repair, there was no need of a change—she left nothing to the pleasure of variety. There appeared to be an inexhaustible store of the same material in a certain capacious drawer; did an elbow give out, a new sleeve instantly supplied its place—did I happen to realize the ancient saying: "There's many a slip 'twixt the cup and the lip," and make my lap the recipient of some of the goodies provided for us at our entertainments, the soiled front breadth disappeared, and was replaced by another, fresh and new—did the waist grow short, it was made over again—there verily seemed to be no end to the dress; I came to the conclusion that blue Circassian was the most ugly material ever invented, and often found myself calculating how many yards there might be left.

My school hats always looked the worse for wear, and my Sunday ones were not much better; but once my mother took me to the city, and bought me, for school, a far handsomer hat than I had hitherto worn for best, and a still better one for great occasions. Here I, who scarcely ever looked decent about the upper story, actually had two new hats at once! The best one, I remember, was a round gipsy flat, then altogether the fashion; and the first Sunday I put it on I made a perfect fool of myself by twisting my hair in strings, intended to pass for natural ringlets, and allowing said strings to hang all around beneath the brim of my hat. Mamma was sick and confined to her room, and I managed to appear at church with this ridiculous head-gear. People certainly stared a little, but this my vanity easily converted into looks of admiration directed towards my new hat, and perhaps also my improved beauty—and came home more full of self-complacency than ever.

I have before mentioned that beyond the house there was a large fruit-garden, respecting which, my father's orders were especially strict. He expressly forbade our touching any of the fruit unless he gave us permission; and nothing made him more angry than to have any gathered before it was quite ripe. It certainly requires a child whose principle of honesty is a very strong one, to pass every day in full view of an endless bed of ripening strawberries, whose uncommon size and luscious hue offered so many temptations. But bad as I was, I think I was generally pretty honest, and resisted the temptation to the best of my ability.

Ella Rodman

CHAPTER V

I think I was about five years old, when one bright May morning my brother Henry received especial instructions to be careful of me, and see that I fell into no mischief on the occasion of my first day at school. The luncheon-basket was packed with twice the usual quantity of sandwiches, into which Mammy slyly tucked a small paper of sweet things as a sort of comforter, with repeated injunctions to Henry not to make a mistake and confiscate them for his own private use. A superfluous caution—for Henry was the most generous little fellow that ever lived; and was far more likely to fall short himself than that others should suffer through him. Both Jane and Mammy kissed me repeatedly. I had on a new dress of light, spotted calico, and a straw hat, with a green ribbon, and a deep green silk cape—underneath the binding of my apron a small handkerchief had been carefully pinned—a small blue-covered book, and a slate with a long, sharp-pointed pencil tied on with a red cord, were placed in my hands; and from these ominous preparations, and the uncommon kindness of every one around, I concluded that I was at last to meet with some adventure—perhaps to suffer martyrdom of some kind or other.

Poor Jane! My great passion was for beads, and when she perceived, from various indications, that I was not exactly pleased with the change, she ran up stairs, hastily loosened a whole string from a cherished necklace, and returning quickly, slipped them into my hand. My mother also came into the nursery to see that I was perfectly neat, kissed me affectionately as she whispered to me to be a good girl and learn to read, and with a strange, undefined sensation at my heart, I found myself in the street with my hand fast locked in that of Henry. It was that lovely season of the year when the fruit-trees are all in bloom; and the sweet, flower-laden breeze, the busy hum of human life that rose around, and the bounding, restless spirit of childhood, made me shrink from the bondage I was about to enter.

The school-house was a very pretty cottage with a trellised front of bean-vines and honeysuckle; and when I entered I found, to my great surprise, that Miss Sewell, the teacher, looked very much like other people. There were two moderate-sized rooms, opening into each other, in one of which Mr. Sewell superintended several desks of unruly boys—in the other, his daughter directed the studies of about twenty little girls. There were some large girls seated at the desks, who appeared to me so very antiquated that I was almost afraid to hazard an idea respecting their ages; and had I been asked how old they were, should probably have replied 'at least fifty;' although I do not now suppose the eldest was more than fourteen.

Rather stunned by the buzz and noise of the classes reciting, and very much puzzled as to my own probable destiny, I began to climb the hill of knowledge. I said my letters; and Miss Sewell, having found that I knew them pretty well, (thanks to Mammy's patient teaching), allowed me to spell in *a-b, ab*, and *b-a, ba*, and set me some straight marks on my slate. I met with nothing remarkable during my first day at school; and on my return informed Mammy, as the result of my studies, that two and one make four. Nor could I be persuaded to the contrary; for, although I had been taught by the old nurse to count as far as ten, on being examined by Miss Sewell, either bashfulness or obstinacy prevented me from displaying the extent of my knowledge—and, while endeavoring to explain to me how many one and one make, she had said: "There is one, to begin with; well now, one more makes two," therefore as one made two in this case, I supposed it did in every other.

I learned to love the mild countenance of Miss Sewell, with her plain dark hair and soft eyes, and was never happier then when she was invited to tea; for then I was emancipated from the nursery and placed beside her at table. I dearly loved to take her fruit and flowers; and white lilies, roses, honey-suckles, and the most admired productions of our garden were daily laid on Miss Sewell's table. For rewards we had a great many wide, bright-colored ribbons, which were tied upon our arms, that every one might see them as we went home; and she who could boast a variety of ribbons was known to have been perfect in all her lessons. Those who had fallen into disgrace were distinguished by a broad band passed around the head, on the front of which was written in large characters the name of the misdemeanor.

One morning I had been rather negligent, and, having my suspicions as to the consequence, told Mammy of my fears, and my dread of the disgrace. The old nurse's anger even exceeded mine; she declared that her child should not be treated so, and advised me to snatch it off and tear it to pieces. I went to school, not having exactly made up my mind whether to follow this advice or not; but my afternoon lessons fully made up for the deficiency of the morning, and I escaped the dreaded punishment. I had gone with several companions to the closet in which we deposited our hats and shawls, and while engaged in the process of robing, I heard a very loud voice talking in great excitement, and one which I immediately recognised. I overheard Mammy exclaiming: "Where is my child? Has she got that horrid thing on her head? I want to take it off before she goes home."

Blushing with mortification, as I noticed the tittering of the school-girls, called forth by the loud tone and strange figure of the old nurse, who had rushed into the room in her usual attire of short-gown and petticoat, I came hastily forward, and was immediately seized by Mammy, who exclaimed in surprise: "Why, I though you said you were going to have that thing on your head! I was determined that no child of mine should wear it, so I came after you to take it off."

Mammy was one of the most independent persons I ever saw; she cared for no one's frown, and poured forth the whole love of her warm Irish heart upon us—tormenting and troublesome as we were. Sometimes she sung to us of "Acushla machree" and "Mavourneen," and Mammy's Irish songs were especial favorites with the young fry of the nursery. When we were particularly obstreperous, she threatened to go away and leave us, and never come back again; a threat which always produced copious showers of tears, and promises of better behavior. Often have I watched her in dismay as she dressed herself to go out—fearful that she would really put her threat in execution, especially as conscience whispered that I deserved it. At such times, nothing pacified me except the deposit of her spectacles; when once the case was lodged in my possession, I felt sure of Mammy—knowing that she could not stay long without them. Sometimes she would tell us of her life in Ireland; but no act did she more bitterly deplore than her marriage; complaining that the object of her choice was far from what he appeared to be when she married him—and further observing that as he turned out a very bad speculation, and never gave her anything but a thimble, she wisely left him to his own society, and emigrated to America.

Mammy very often kept the key of the fruit-garden; and as she never yielded it to our entreaties, the ever-ready Fred formed a conspiracy one Sunday afternoon, in which, I am sorry to say, I took a very conspicuous part—the object of

Ella Rodman

which was to purloin the key, and enjoy at last this long-coveted, forbidden pleasure. Fred actually succeeded in abstracting it from Mammy's capacious pocket, and in high glee we proceeded to the garden. It was in the time of peaches; there hung the lucious fruit in such profusion, that the trees were almost borne down by its weight. We ate till we could eat no longer; and then, happening to see two or three men passing along, we threw some over the fence to them. They, in return, threw us some pennies; and, delighted with the success of our frolic, we continued to throw and receive, until startled by a most unwelcome apparition. There, at the foot of the tree, stood Mammy—her face expressing the utmost astonishment and indignation, and her hands extended to seize us. She had watched our manoeuvres from one of the windows, and astonishment at our boldness and ingenuity kept her for sometime a silent spectator. But Mammy was not apt to be *silent* long while witnessing our misdeeds; and in an incredible short space of time she gained the use of both her feet and her tongue. Our companions caught a glimpse of flying drapery rapidly advancing, and rather suddenly made their retreat; while we, now trembling, detected culprits, took up a line of march for the house.

Not so, Fred; defying Mammy to capture him, and laughing at her dismay, he started off on a run, and she after him in full pursuit. We watched the chase from the nursery-window; and as Fred was none of the thinnest, and Mammy somewhat resembled a meal-bag with a string tied round the middle, it proved to be quite exciting. But it was brought to an untimely end by the apparition of a pair of spectacles over the fence; said spectacles being the undisputed property of a middle-aged gentleman—a bachelor, who, we suspected, always stayed home from church on Sunday afternoons to keep the neighbors in order. With horror-stricken eyes he had beheld only the latter part of the scene, and conceiving the old nurse to be as bad as her rebellious charge, he called out from his garden, which communicated with ours:

"My good woman, do you know that this is Sunday?—Depend upon it, a person of your years would feel much better to be quietly reading in your own apartment, than racing about the garden in this unseemly manner."

Poor Mammy! she was well aware of this before; flushed, heated, and almost overcome with fatigue, she looked the very picture of uncomfortableness; and this last aggravation increased the feeling to a tenfold degree. At that moment, Fred, unconsciously, stumbled into her very arms; she looked up—the spectacles had disappeared—and convinced of this fact, she bore him in triumph to the nursery.

We had all expected personal chastisement, at the very least, but we were thrown into a greater degree of horror and dismay than could well be conceived; Mammy placed her spectacles in her pocket, collected her valuables, and put on her hat and things, to take passage for Ireland. We hung about her in every attitude of entreaty—acknowledged our misdemeanors, promised amendment, and an entire confession of all the sins we had ever perpetrated. I do think we must have remained upon our knees at least half an hour; never had Mammy seemed so hard-hearted before, and we began to think that she might be in earnest after all. We begged her to whip us—lock us up—anything but leave us; and at last she relented. She told us that she considered us the most abandoned children that ever were born; and wished that she had two additional eyes at the back of her head to watch our movements. We promised to spend the afternoon in learning hymns and verses; and Mammy, having taken her position in the large easy-chair, with a footstool at her feet, tied Fred to one of the legs, as he sat on a low bench at her side, and made us all study. We succeeded pretty well; although considerably terrified at the sharp looks which Mammy from time to time bestowed upon us.

In the evening came the promised confession; and both

Ella Rodman

Mammy and Jane were rendered almost dumb by these dreadful instances of depravity. Such secret and unsuspected visits to the store-room pantry—such conspiracies against locks and bolts—such scaling of walls, and climbing in at windows, were never heard of before. I rather suspected Fred to have drawn upon his imagination for instances of the marvellous, for such adventures as he related never could have been met with; but Mammy and Jane believed it all. At the conclusion, the old nurse seemed very much disposed to punish us at once for all these united misdemeanors—and was only prevented by our remonstrating upon the plea of a voluntary confession.

That night I lay awake, pretending to sleep, and heard Mammy and her satellite discussing our conduct in all its enormity. Considerably influenced by their unaffected horror and astonishment, the thought for the first time rushed upon my mind, that perhaps I might be much worse than other people. It troubled me considerably; I found it impossible to sleep, and following a good impulse, I crept softly out of bed, and falling on my knees before Mammy, whispered to her to pray for me. There must have been a very different expression on my countenance from its usual one; for I afterwards heard the old nurse tell Jane that I reminded her of an angel. I felt utterly miserable; and sobbing convulsively, I begged Mammy to pray, not that I might have a new heart, but that I might live a great while. I had begun to fear speedy punishment for my misdemeanors. The old nurse, (although a really pious woman), seemed quite at a loss how to proceed; and Jane, coming forward, took me kindly by the hand, and reasoned with me on my conduct with all the wisdom of riper years and a higher education. After convincing me that I should ask, not for an increased number of years, but for a new heart and temper, she knelt down with me and repeated the Lord's prayer.

The scene is indelibly impressed upon my memory; for

although I have since witnessed scenes containing more stage effect, and quite as melting, I never in my life remember to have been so affected as, with Jane's arm around me, and the light of the nursery-lamp shining upon our kneeling figures, I distinctly heard Mammy's sobs, as she repeated each word with a peculiar intonation of reverence. I felt a respect for the young girl ever afterwards; and as I clasped my arms about her neck and pressed a warm kiss on her cheek, as I bade her good-night, the tone of my voice must have been unusually tender—for I saw tears come into her eyes as she asked Mammy if she was not afraid, from my flushed cheeks, that I had some fever. Although petulant, and even violent when roused, I had a warm, loving heart, capable of the most unbounded affection; and from that time forth Jane and I never had a single dispute. She had appeared to me in a new light on that Sabbath eve; and with my hand locked in hers, I fell into a sweet, dreamy sleep.

Ella Rodman

CHAPTER VI

One of my great troubles, and one too which I regarded in a pretty serious light, was the obeisance I had been taught to make on meeting "the minister's wife." I never came within view of this formidable personage that I did not hesitate and tremble; while I looked wildly around, in the vain hope of discovering a place of refuge. After performing my awkward courtesy, I usually hastened on as fast as possible, being oppressed with a most uncomfortable sensation of awe in the presence of Mrs. Eylton. This was occasioned by the quiet observance which I, like other children, took of the conduct of those around me. Everything in the house seemed to be at her command; if Mrs. Eylton sent for a thing she must have it immediately; and I drew my conclusions that "the minister's wife" was a sort of petty sovereign, placed over the town or village in which she resided, and that all we possessed was held under her.

Almost every day brought a request from Mrs. Eylton for the loan of some article in our possession; a repetition of which would naturally lead one to conclude that ministers merely procured a house, and then depended for everything else on the charity of the public. This borrowing mania appeared to gather strength from indulgence, for none of the neighbors would refuse, whatever the article might be; and our waffle-iron, toasting-fork, Dutch-oven, bake-pan, and rolling-pin were frequently from home on visits of a week's duration. On sending for our muffin-rings or cake-pans, we often received a message to be expeditious in our manufactures; that Mrs. Eylton could spare them for a day or so, "but wanted to use them again very shortly." Our parents would buy such conveniences, send them to the kitchen of Mrs. Eylton, and borrow them from time to time, if in perfect accordance with that lady's convenience. She would even borrow her neighbor's servants, and often at very inconvenient times. Jane had often been sent for to take care of the children; and the usual request came one afternoon that seemed to me stamped with most remarkable events.

We were in a kind of sitting-room on the ground-floor, and my father sat writing at a small table near the window. A servant entered with the announcement: "Mrs. Eylton, ma'am, wants to borrow Jane."

An expression of vexation crossed my mother's countenance as she remarked: "I do not know how I can possibly spare Jane this afternoon; Mammy has gone out, and I do not feel inclined to attend to the children myself."

My father looked up from his writing as he observed: "Nor do I see the necessity of your being troubled with them, Laura."

"Not see the necessity!" exclaimed my mother, "How can I refuse the wife of our minister? I would be willing to put up with some inconvenience for Mr. Eylton's sake. Poor man! he has a hard time of it, with his talents and refinement."

"No doubt he has," said my father, pityingly; then, in a more merry tone, he added: "But can you think of no other alternative, Laura, than disobliging Mrs. Eylton, if you object to this juvenile infliction for a whole long summer's afternoon?"

Ella Rodman

My father was of a bolder, more determined character than my mother, and had, withal, a spice of fun in his composition; and the expression of his eyes now rendered her apprehensive of some sudden scheme that might create a feeling of justifiable anger in Mrs. Eylton.

"Dearest Arthur!" she exclaimed beseechingly, as she placed a soft hand on his shoulder, "Do not, I beseech of you, put in execution any outlandish plan respecting Mrs. Eylton!—Do let Jane go as usual; for she is not one to understand a joke, I can assure you—she will be offended by it."

"And pray, madam," asked my father, with assumed gravity, "what has led you to suppose that I intended making Mrs. Eylton the subject of a joke? Away with you," he continued, with a mischievous look at those pleading eyes, "Away with you, and let me do as I choose."

Turning to the servant, he asked: "Mrs. Eylton has, I believe, requested the loan of other articles besides our domestics—has she ever sent to borrow any of the children?"

"Indeed, and she has not, sir," replied the girl, with difficulty repressing a laugh.

"Well then," said he, "we will now send her both the article she requested, and some articles which she did not request. Tell Jane to be ready to go to Mrs. Eylton's with the children."

"Yes sir," and the servant departed to execute her commission.

"Arthur!" remonstrated my mother.

"Not a word!" said my father gaily. "Children," he continued, "do you wish to go? What says my madcap, Amy?"

Madcap Amy, for once in her life, said nothing—being too much awed and astonished to reply. To think that I should actually enter the house, and be face to face with the formidable Mrs. Eylton? The idea was appalling; and for sometime I sat biting my nails in thoughful silence. It was so sudden, it had always appeared to me that a great deal must be gone through with—a great many different degrees of intimacy surmounted, before I should ever find myself within the house of Mrs. Eylton; but here was I, without the least warning, to be transformed from the bashful child, who made no sign of recognition save an awkward courtesy, into the regular visitor—and for a whole afternoon! No wonder I took so long to deliberate. Though not particularly remark-able for bashfulness or timidity at home, and despite a character for violence in, "fighting my own battles," to assert some infringed right, I absolutely trembled at the idea of encountering strangers; and this visit to Mrs. Eylton's appeared, to my excited mind, like thrusting myself into the enemy's quarters.

But then curiosity rose up in all its powers, to baffle my fear; I did *so* want to see how the house looked inside, and whether they really had anything that was not borrowed! And then who knows, thought I, but what Mrs. Eylton will show me the inside of some of her drawers? I dare say she has a great many pretty things. There was nothing which gave me greater delight than looking into other people's drawers, and turning over those remnants of various things which are stored away in most houses—in many for the mere love of hoarding. Mamma would sometimes allow me to arrange certain little drawers containing jewelry, ribbons, and odds and ends. But the charmed room in our house was one that was always kept locked, and, from the circumstance of a green ribbon being attached to the key, we called it "the green-ribbon room."

Dear me! what a collection that room contained. There were

Ella Rodman

several large trunks that nearly covered the floor, besides boxes, and bags, and bundles; and these were filled with cast-off clothes, silks, ribbons, and bunches of artificial flowers and feathers. The room was not very often opened; it was at the very top of the house, and lighted by a large dormar-window; but as soon as mamma mounted the stairs, with the key in her hand, the alarm was given: "Quick! mother is going to the green-ribbon room!" and mamma's ears were immediately refreshed by the sound of numerous little feet moving up stairs at locomotive speed, with the ostensible purpose of assisting her in her researches—but in reality, to be getting in her way, and begging for everything we saw. It was, "Mamma, mayn't we have this?" or, "mayn't we have that?" or "Do say yes, just this once; and we'll never ask you for anything again as long as we live—never," a promise faithfully kept till next time.

Mamma sometimes tried to go up very softly, in order to elude our vigilance; but it wouldn't do. She often wondered how we found out that that she was there, but we seldom missed an opportunity. Now and then a dear little pitcher, or a vase of cream-colored ground with a wreath of faint pink roses traced around it, or a cluster of bright-colored flowers in the centre, arrested our attention, and called forth rhapsodies of admiration. I supposed that everybody had just such a room; and it was very probable, I thought, that Mrs. Eylton might chance to open hers during our visit. Therefore I decided that, notwithstanding my terror of the lady, a greater amount of pleasure might be obtained by going there, than by staying at home.

So Jane, with her own trim person as neat as possible, bore off her charges to the nursery, in order, as she said, "to make us fit to be seen." "Mrs. Eylton might see this," or "notice that," and I felt uncomfortably convinced that Mrs. Eylton must possess the sharpest pair of eyes it had ever been my misfortune to encounter. Finally, we set off; I remember being dressed in a white frock, with a broad sash, and experiencing a consciousness of looking remarkably well, in spite of my hair—which, having obstinately repulsed all Jane's advances with tongs and curl-papers, was suffered to remain in all its native straightness.

It was summer, and a multiflora rose-vine, which extended over the front of the parsonage, was then in full flower; while, as we mounted the steps, I distinguished through the green blind door glimpses of a pleasant-looking garden beyond. We entered the back parlor, where sat Mrs. Eylton attired for a walk, and surrounded by three children, all younger than myself. The minister's lady did not appear quite so formidable on a close survey; though the aspect of her countenance was by no means promising, as her eye fell upon us.

"Well, Jane," she commenced, in the tone of one who felt herself injured, "you have kept me waiting some time—how is this? Punctuality is a virtue very becoming in a young person."

Jane looked exceedingly disconcerted at this address; but at length she replied, that "she could not get the children ready before."

"*The children!*" repeated Mrs. Eylton; while, young as I was, I plainly read in her countenance, "What possessed you to bring *them* here?"

"Yes ma'am," replied Jane, gathering more courage as she proceeded, "Mrs. Chesbury sent them with me to spend the afternoon. She had no one to attend to them at home."

In the meantime I became aware, as I glanced around the room, that the prospect for the afternoon promised very little amusement. Mrs. Eylton soon after left us, telling Jane to be very careful that we got into no mischief; and, with, a feeling of disappointment, I saw the door close behind her. In my scenting of the apartment I became very much struck with the appearance of a curious looking little work-stand, containing three small drawers. Immediately my imagination was at work upon their contents; and I determined, if possible, to satisfy my curiosity. Mrs. Eylton had departed without making any provision for our amusement, and I saw no reason why I should not examine the drawers—especially if I handled things carefully, and put them all back again. Probably they were in disorder, and then what a pleasant surprise it would be for Mrs. Eylton to find them all neatly arranged on her return!

Jane now proposed walking in the garden; and to avoid suspicion, I joined the party for the present. There were a great many flower-beds, very prettily laid out; and at the end of a wide path stood a pleasant little summer-house, half-buried in vines. We established ourselves there, from whence we could view the whole garden; and with a pretence of looking again at the flowers, I soon made my escape, and returned to the house. A wide glass-door opened from the back room into the garden, and carefully closing this, I approached the table and attempted to open the drawers. I tried the first one,—it was locked; the second,—and met with no better success. Almost in despair, I placed my hands on the third, and that finally yielded to my efforts. I beheld heterogeneous rows of pins, papers of needles, &c., and was about to shut it in disappointment, when my glance fell on a small box. Small, mysterious-looking boxes always possessed a talismanic attraction in my eyes; and the next moment I was busily at work examining the contents. The round lid lifted, I found my gaze irresistibly fascinated by a child's face, with fair, curling hair, and azure eyes. But the great beauty lay in its expression; that was so calm, holy, and serene, that I felt insensibly better as I gazed upon it. It was a peculiar face; and I became so wrapt in its contemplation as to lose all hearing of what passed around, until a step sounded close beside me.

I looked up, and fairly trembled with terror and dismay. There stood Mr. Eylton, gazing on me in surprise, as if quite at a loss what to make of the circumstance; but as his eye fell upon the picture, I noticed that an expression of sadness crossed his countenance. Not knowing what to do with myself, and almost ready to sink through the floor with shame, I stood with bowed head and burning cheeks, the very picture of mortification. But there was no trace of anger in Mr. Eylton's tone, as, kindly taking me by the hand, he drew me towards him and asked me my name. I answered as well as I could; and still holding the picture, remained in silent consternation. Mr. Eylton took it from my hand, and sighed as he bent a deep, loving gaze upon the fair face.

Prompted by a sudden impulse, I raised my eyes to his, as I enquired: "Can you tell me where that little girl is now? I should *so* like to see her!"

"In heaven, I trust," replied Mr. Eylton, while his voice slightly faltered, and a tear stood in his eye. "She was my daughter, Amy—she died some years ago, when very young."

I felt almost ready to cry myself, when told that she was dead, and gazed lingeringly upon the portrait as Mr. Eylton closed the box; and placing it in the drawer, he returned to me again.

"But, my dear child," said he suddenly, "Why did you open the drawer? Do you not know that it was extremely improper?"

"I did *so* want to see what was in it!" was my rejoinder.

Ella Rodman

Mr. Eylton seemed puzzled at first by this reply; but probably perceiving that I had been too much left to myself, he proceeded to explain, in clear and concise words, the nature and tendency of my fault. "This curiosity, my dear child, is an improper state of feeling which should not be indulged in. Suppose," continued he, "that on looking into this drawer, you had perceived some article which you immediately felt a great desire to possess; yielding to the temptation of curiosity would thus lead to the sin of covetousness, and perhaps the crime of theft might be also added. You would reason with yourself that no one had seen you open the drawer, and forgetting the all-seeing Eye which never slumbers, you might conclude that no one would know you took the article which did not belong to you."

The prospect of becoming a thief struck me with horror; and resolving never again to meddle with other people's things, I begged Mr. Eylton to forgive me, and entreated him not to inform Mrs. Eylton of my misdemeanor. He smiled at the anxiety I displayed not to have it known; and then taking a bunch of keys from a box, he proceeded to gratify my curiosity with respect to the other drawers. These amply repaid an investigation; containing numerous toys and trinkets of foreign manufacture, among which were two or three small alabaster images. One represented a beautiful greyhound in a reclining position; there was an Italian image of the Virgin and Child; and some others which I have almost forgotten. I was allowed to examine all these things at my leisure; and when I departed, it was with a firm conviction that Mr. Eylton was far more agreeable than his wife.

Jane soon came in from the summer-house, after an unsuccessful search for me through the garden, and was not a little surprised to find me quietly established with Mr. Eylton. Towards sunset Mrs. Eylton returned; and being graciously dismissed, we went home with the impression that it had been altogether rather a curious visit. But the afternoon dwelt in my memory like a golden gleam; and often I went over, in imagination, that delightful investigation of Mrs. Eylton's drawers.

CHAPTER VII

We were generally besieged with visitors of all descriptions and characters. My parents had one or two poor relations who made long stays at every visit; and being generous, even to a fault, they loaded them with presents at their departure, and invitations to come again. There was one old lady, in particular, who engaged my fancy; she came to see us quite often, and in the family went by the name of "Aunty Patton." Aunty Patton was a widow, with very slender means; and boarded with a married daughter, who had a large family of children, but very little to support them on. Poor Aunty! she fared rather poorly at home, and did *so* seem to enjoy everything. She was particularly fond of fruit-cake; and whenever she came, mamma took particular pains that this should be one of the appliances of the tea-table. She possessed many wealthy acquaintances and relations, and enjoyed visiting around among them very much; praising everything that was set before her, and never contradicting any one. It teemed impossible to put anything on the table which she did not like; everything was "good," and "delightful," and "just what she would have fancied." At length some cousin determined to test her patience; and on one occasion, when the old lady happened to dine there, the dishes, when uncovered, were found to contain nothing but supaun and potatoes.

"I am really sorry, Aunty Patton," began the hostess, "to be able to offer you nothing better for dinner—but sometimes you know"—

"O," said Aunty, with rather a rueful look, "it'll *do*."

Poor Aunty had that very day prepared herself for something uncommonly nice in the way of dinner, and felt a little disappointed; but cousin Emma soon restored her equanimity by a liberal display of fruit-cake and other nice things, which presented themselves on opening the side-board door.

Aunty Patton had mild, winning kind of manners, and became a general favorite in the nursery; probably on account of her always noticing us, and pronouncing us "lovely little creatures." She appeared to me the most heavenly-minded old lady I had ever seen; and I listened, with a species of awe, to the long stories which she loved so dearly to relate about everybody whom she visited. She was very short—not seeming to me much taller than myself—and the cumbrous dress of the period was calculated to make her appear much shorter. She would sit and relate wonderful occurrences which seemed constantly taking place in her daughter's family; one of the children would cut his foot, and for sometime there would be danger of amputation—another urchin would upset a kettle of scalding water on himself, and then he would be laid up for sometime, while mamma turned the green-ribbon room topsy-turvy in her searches after old linen—and once the daughter fell down stairs, and was taken up for dead. They seemed to be an unfortunate family—always meeting with hair-breadth escapes. Aunty Patton's reticule was always well filled with good things on every occasion of her departure; and very often a collection of money was added to the stock.

Mamma sometimes endeavored to enlist our sympathies in benevolent purposes. I remember, on one occasion, when I had been teasing sometime for a new tortoise-shell comb to keep back my hair with, it suddenly entered my head that it

Ella Rodman

would be a well-disposed action to ask for some money to give Aunty Patton.

"Are you willing, Amy, to deny yourself anything," asked mamma, after I had made my request, "in order that I may give this money to Aunty Patton? It is no benevolence in you to ask me to give away money, unless you are willing to do without something in consequence. If I give Aunty Patton the five dollars that your comb will cost, are you willing to do without it?"

"Dear me," thought I, "being good is very expensive." I deliberated for sometime, but finally answered, "No." My mother pressed the subject no farther; but after a while I exclaimed with a comfortable feeling of magnanimity; "Yes, dear mamma, you *may* give Aunty Patton the five dollars—and I'll get *papa* to buy me the comb!"

Mammy was a great judge of character, and when she once made up her mind not to like a person, it was very difficult to make her change her sentiments. My father once brought in a travelling clergyman, who represented himself as very devout and unfortunate; and we all made great efforts to entertain him. He was travelling West, he said, and endeavoring to collect on the road sufficient money to pay his expenses. My father invited him to remain with us a month; and he seemed very much to enjoy the good things so liberally showered upon him—contriving at the same time to render himself so agreeable that he quite won our hearts. Mammy alone remained proof against his insinuations; he paid assiduous court to her, and did his best to remove this unfavorable impression, but the old nurse remained immovable.

He once asked her for the key to the fruit-garden, when my parents were both out; but Mammy stedfastly refused him. "She had orders," she said, "not to let the key go out of her possession, and she didn't intend to now." The wandering clergyman departed quite enraged; and reported proceedings as soon as my father returned. He was very much displeased at Mammy's obstinacy, and spoke quite warmly on the subject; but the old nurse replied that "she didn't know but he might make off with half the fruit in the garden—she didn't like the man's looks at any rate."

I had then in my possession a little morocco pocket-book, a treasured article, which I valued above all my other worldly goods. Sometime before Christmas, I had observed it in a a shop-window with passionate admiration; and on my return home, I threw out various hints and inuendoes—scarcely hoping that they would be attended to. They were, however; for on examining my stocking on the eventful morning, the long-coveted pocket-book was found sticking in the toe— and what was still better, well supplied with contents. I was in ecstasy for sometime after; but wishing to do something to signalize myself, I now placed it in the hands of the Rev. Mr. Motley for safe keeping.

"Mark my words," said Mammy prophetically, "you'll never see a sign of that pocket-book again."

Alas! her words were but too true; circumstances came to light not very favorable to the character of our visitor; and that very night the Rev. Mr. Motley secretly decamped— mentioning in a note left behind, that unlooked-for events had hastened his departure. My little pocket-book accompanied him, as he quite forgot to return it; and Mammy's triumph was almost as provoking as the loss. She had, however, with characteristic caution, abstracted whatever money it contained; and the reflection that the reverend gentleman had not gained much, gave her considerable pleasure. The lesson taught me not to trust strangers again too readily, and my father imbibed somewhat of a prejudice against traveling clergymen in distress. Rev. Mr. Motley

Ella Rodman

was never again heard of.

We once had a visit from a Captain Vardell, an acquaintance of my father's, who had married a Spanish woman. This Captain had spent much of his time at sea; roving about from place to place, until at length he settled down for some years in Spain. He had no relations in America, and but little money, so that of course my father's house, the usual refuge of the needy and distressed, was at once his destination. He appeared to us an indolent, good-natured kind of a man, and his wife resembled him in the former quality, though quite deficient in the latter. She could not speak a word of English, and would scold and rail at her husband in Spanish for hours together. We did not understand what she said, but we knew, by the flashing of those great black eyes and her animated gestures, that her words were not words of love. She was a large woman, with straight, black hair, that seemed to be always hanging about her face, and rather handsome features. She spent most of her time in playing jackstraws with us, or else lounging on the sofa; muttering in rapid succession the words of a small prayer-book, which Captain Vardell told us she always carried about her, as it had been consecrated and given to her by a Spanish priest. She appeared to us very much like a great overgrown baby; manifesting the most childish delight on winning a game, and equally angry when defeated. Once, when in extreme good-humor, she shewed us how to make beads resembling coral, from a certain paste which she manufactured; but we never could extract from her the names of the materials, and were obliged to content ourselves with making them under her direction.

Mrs. Vardell was so extremely lazy that she would never stoop to pick up anything she had dropped. If her handkerchief or prayer-book fell to the floor, she made motions for us to bring them to her; and when we sometimes mischievously pretended not to understand these signs, she would let the article remain until some one restored it to her. She never seemed to experience the least emotion of gratitude, and received all favors as a natural right. She was an extremely troublesome, exacting visitor, and we were not at all sorry when the time of her departure arrived.

My father had exerted himself on their behalf, and at the end of their visit handed Captain Vardell a handsome sum of money, collected from among his merchant friends and acquaintances. People were much more liberal then than now, and the case of the Vardells did not fail to call forth their sympathy and generosity. The Spanish lady made her adieus, if so they could be called, with an easy indifference —apparently considering her fellow-mortals as machines invented for her sole use and benefit. Captain Vardell presented us children with a handsome collection of shells, picked up on foreign shores during his numerous voyages; and some of them were very rare and beautiful. Most of them had a delicate pink tinge, like the outer leaves of a just-blown rose; and we amused ourselves fur a long time by arranging them in a glass-case which my father gave us for the purpose.

Among our visitors was an aunt of my mother's who lived in Waterford, Connecticut; and being a widow, with quite a large farm to attend to, her visits were never of long duration. I became very much attached to her, for she often entertained us with long stories about the Revolution and the aggressions of the British soldiers—about which you shall hear when I come to tell you of the long visit I made there one summer. Aunt Henshaw was very proud of her farm and farming operations; her cattle and vegetables had several times won the prize at agricultural fairs, and she boasted that her land produced more than any of her neighbors'; who, being men, were of course expected to be more accomplished in such matters. She appeared to delight in giving away things, and seldom made us a visit without

Ella Rodman

bringing something of her own raising. These little presents my father always repaid tenfold; and Aunt Henshaw departed without a new gown or hat, or something to show when she got home. I believe that we generally anticipated more pleasure from her visits than from any of the numerous friends who often favored us with their company.

But Aunt Henshaw, I must confess, won my heart less by her own individual merits than a present she once made me, which actually appeared to me like a windfall from the skies. I was always inordinately fond of reading, and my predelictions for fairy tales amounted to an actual passion. When Mammy and Jane's ingenuity had been exhausted in framing instances of the marvellous for my special gratification, I would often fold my hands before my face, to shut out all actual scenes, and thus sit and dream of wonderful adventures with fairies, witches, and enchanted princesses. I was always happier in a reverie than in the company of others—my own ideals I could make as I chose—the real I must take as I found it. Castle-building is a pleasant but dangerous occupation; had I not been so much of an enthusiast, a day-dreamer, it would have been better for my happiness.

But to return to Aunt Henshaw and her present. Some school-mate one day told me of the varied wonders contained in the "Arabian Kights." My imagination, always excitable, became worked up to a high pitch by tales of diamond caverns, flying horses, and mysterious Baloons under ground. If I went to sleep, it was to dream of gardens more beautiful than Paradise itself—of cooling fountains springing up at every step—of all sorts of impossible fruits growing just where you wanted them—and lamps and songs that gratified every wish. At length I could bear these tantalizing visions of unattainable pleasure no longer; I put on my bonnet and determined to go the whole rounds of the village until I met with some success. People wondered what ailed me that afternoon; I bolted directly into a room—asked if they had the Arabian Nights—and, on being answered in the negative, went out as expeditiously as I had gone in, and tried another acquaintance. I was not easily daunted, and took each one in succession, but all to no purpose; I returned home, fairly sick with disappointment, and hope delayed.

The very next day Aunt Henshaw came down on a visit; and placing in my hands an old-looking, leather-covered book, observed, "I happened to come across this stowed away in an old chest, Amy, and knowing your fondness for fairy tales, I have brought it for you to read."

I scarcely heard what she said; I had glanced at the book, and on seeing "Arabian Nights" traced in large gilt letters, the ground seemed swimming before me, and I could scarcely contain my senses. Seizing the beloved book, I made my escape as quickly as possible; and mounting up to the cupola, a tiny room with glass sides, that commanded a view of the country round, I effectually secured myself against interruption, and soon became fascinated out of all remembrance. The day waned into evening—the shadows deepened around —I remember fixing my eyes on a brilliant star that seemed to come closer and closer, until it assumed a strangely beautiful form, and I lost all consciousness.

In the meantime a strict search for me had been going on below. They began to be alarmed at my continued absence; and after examining every room, the garden, and every spot on the premises, they sent around the neighborhood. I was known to be extremely fond of visiting, and every acquaintance was interrogated in turn—of course, without success. No one had thought of the cupola, and mamma was getting fairly frightened; when Mammy took a light, and on ascending to my dormitory, discovered me fast asleep, with the book tightly clasped to my bosom.

Ella Rodman

It afterwards yielded the boys as much delight as it had me; Fred, in particular, had a notion of trying experiments upon the plan there laid out. He had sat one afternoon for sometime with the book in his hands—apparently resolving some problem in his own mind; Mammy was stooping over the nursery fire, when she was suddenly startled by an unexpected shower of water sprinkled over her head and neck—Fred at the same time exclaiming, in a tone that seemed to doubt not: "I command you instantly to turn into a coal black mare!"

"I don't know what would become of you, you good-for-naught, if I did!" returned Mammy.

Some years later I read "The Children of the Abbey," and this opened a new field of thought. My dreams, instead of being peopled with fairies and genii, were now filled with distressed damsels who met with all sorts of persecutions and Quixotic adventures, and finally ended where they should have commenced.

CHAPTER VIII

I had a boy-lover who always selected me as his partner in all our plays, and kept me in pointers with blue ribbons attached to them, to point out the towns on the large map in the school-room. Charles Tracy was about my own age, but in disposition and taste he resembled my brother Henry, and the two were quite inseparable; while his sister Ellen and I formed an acquaintance through the fence by displaying our dolls to each other—and this was the beginning of an intimacy that lasted a long time for children's friendships.

Ellen possessed a charm which often caused me to experience the uncomfortable sensation of envy; her hair fell in long, golden-colored ringlets upon her neck and shoulders, and these same curls seemed to shake about so nicely whenever she moved her head. I sometimes thought that Ellen shook them about much more than was absolutely necessary; but at the same time they excited my warmest admiration. I felt as though I could do anything—go through with all sorts of difficulties to have my hair curl naturally; and with a feeling of unspeakable rapture I listened to Ellen one day as she told me in a mysterious whisper that the nurse had said eating crusts made her hair curl.

Eating crusts! What a discovery!—I immediately felt ready to eat all the crusts in our house and every one else's. I bribed the children to deliver up all their crusts to me, and

Ella Rodman

commenced eating them with a voracity that excited the surprise of all the nursery inmates. But already, in perspective, I beheld my head adorned with long, glossy curls, and I persevered, despite the laughter I excited. I devoured crusts by the wholesale, but alas! no waving locks rewarded my patient toil; and at length I had the pleasure of hearing that the crust business was a fable, invented by Ellen's nurse to induce that young lady to finish her odds and ends of bread, which she was very much disposed to scatter about the nursery. It was cruel, after being elevated to such a pinnacle of happiness, to find my hopes thus rudely dashed to the ground; and my hair seemed straighter than ever, from contrast with what I had expected it to be. Ellen was prevented from wasting her crusts, and so far it was well; but the nurse lost by her falsehood whatever respect I may have had for her—a loss which she perhaps did not regard as such, or indeed trouble herself at all about—but even a child's good opinion is something.

I was very much inclined to be fleshy—too much so, I thought, for beauty of figure; and this was another great annoyance. People in speaking of us, always used to say: "What fine large children!" until I hated the very sound of it, and wished most earnestly for Ellen's light, fairy-like figure. I once resolved to starve myself into growing thin; and, to Mammy's great surprise, refused to taste the dinner she handed me, and resolutely persisted in going to bed without my supper. Mammy, good old soul! watched me narrowly, not having been let into the secret of my laudable resolve; and while she supposed that I had fallen into a restless slumber, I was in reality tossing about on my trundle bed, suffering the tantalizing pains of hunger. I remonstrated with myself in vain; heard all the *pros* and *cons* on both sides in this perplexing case of vanity *vs.* appetite, and finally resolved to satisfy my hunger, cost what it would.

But how to do this was the next question. Enticing slices of bread and butter kept dancing before my eyes; and at length, when I heard the snore which announced Mammy's departure to the land of dreams, I rose as quietly as possible, and descended on a foraging expedition to the pantry. How very nice everything did look! I stood for a moment feasting my eyes with the sight, but oh, ill-timed delay! I had not tasted a single morsel, when a low whisper fell upon my ear, and on turning, I beheld Mammy gazing on me rather fearfully, while at her elbow stood Jane in night-gown and cap, who was violently rubbing her eyes in order to clear away the fancied mist, and thus convince herself that it was really the veritable *me* who was about to perform such an unheroine-like part.

This discovery seemed to me exactly like those tantalizing dreams in which you are sitting down at a table covered with everything nice, but before you have time to taste anything your visions are rudely dispelled, and you wake and look in vain for the tempting paraphernalia. I once bore this in mind after being several times teased in this manner; and resolving not to be so deceived again, I succeeded in regaling myself with a mince-pie—which appeared to me quite in the light of a triumph. I now cast about me for some means to escape from this disagreeable dilemma; and having heard Mammy whisper to Jane: "How very wild she looks!" I found that they supposed me to be walking in my sleep, a practice to which I was somewhat addicted; and not seeing why sleep-walkers should not direct their course to the cupboard as well as anywhere else, I boldly seized a loaf and commenced an attack upon it.

"Let us wait and see what she will do," whispered Mammy.

"It is very evident what she will do, now that she has the loaf in her hands," replied Jane in a sleepy tone. "I do not believe that she is asleep at all, but just as wide awake as we are. I have read a story somewhere," she continued, "of a French

Ella Rodman

girl who succeeded in persuading people that she lived without eating; but at last some one watched the girl closely, and one night discovered her at the pantry, regaling herself with cold chicken sufficiently to go without eating for a week. Now, Miss Amy has eaten neither dinner nor supper, and she may be imitating the French girl, in order to be made a fuss with. I will speak to her and see."

"Not for the world!" exclaimed Mammy in terror, as she grasped the more enterprising Jane. "Do not touch her—for I have heard of its killing people to be awakened suddenly while in this state."

Jane obeyed, although her face still wore an incredulous expression; and I continued eating, looking as wild as possible all the time. The nursery-maid began at length to fear that I would put an end to my own life, if not spoken to; but Mammy still objected—murmuring as she watched my voracious performances; "Poor child! how hungry she must have been to come down and eat in her sleep! I wonder why she refused her tea?"

After a while, however, I became more sleepy than hungry; and Mammy and Jane kindly conveyed me back to my little bed, where I slept soundly till morning. I was not destined to reap much glory from this escapade—not even the glory of being a sleep-walker; for Jane, looking me steadily in the face, said: "Now, Miss Amy, I wish you to tell me truly whether you were asleep last night, when you went down into the pantry and devoured almost a whole loaf of bread! Now be a good girl, and tell the truth, for you frightened us very much."

At first I pretended stupidity, and inquired, "what pantry?" and "what bread?" but Jane soon discovered that I knew very well; and while she looked at me so searchingly I could not possibly frame a plausible story—so, from sheer necessity, I told the whole truth, "and nothing but the truth." My curious attempt at getting thin excited great amusement; but Mammy told me that she knew of a better way than that, which was to run up and down stairs as much as possible. I followed her advice until I became tired of it; and during that period I was universally acknowledged to be the most obliging child in the house, for I was quite indefatigable in running on other people's errands. I became discouraged, though, when I found that I remained as fat as ever; and began tasking my brain for some other expedient.

I had gone to Ellen Tracy's to enjoy a holiday; and, quite mad with spirits, we roamed hither and thither, scarcely knowing what to do with ourselves. At length Ellen proposed that we should go to "the boys' room," and go we accordingly did. We would have recognized it as the sanctum of two or three noisy urchins of the male gender, even had we not known it beforehand. On the dressing-table stood a top, half-a-dozen marbles, and a fishing-line; while the walls displayed various quaint devices of their own drawing. There was a something which, Ellen informed us, was intended for a ghost; but if so, he had a most undue proportion of flesh on his bones, and looked far more like a giant. We concluded to equip ourselves in male attire, for the sake of variety—being heartily tired of frocks and petticoats; and Ellen's pretty curls having been tucked up under a round cap, she looked so fascinating that I felt quite ambitious to rival her—but in attempting to draw on one of Charles' jackets, I found that it would not meet round my waist. Oh, mortification unspeakable! to find myself larger around the waist than a boy a whole year my senior! I could scarcely refrain from bursting into tears; forgetting that I belonged to the dumpling order, while Charles was as slender and straight as a young birch tree. My pleasure for that day was gone; in vain Ellen displayed her whole stock of worldly possessions to tempt my admiration. I scarcely bestowed a look on anything, and returned home perfectly miserable.

Ella Rodman

For days I kept my ears wide open in hopes of catching something that might relieve my distress, and at length I met with some success. I overheard a visitor telling my mother of some young lady, whose figure they had been admiring, that she was nothing at all without her corsets—a complete dumpling; and then followed a long digression on the impropriety of imposing upon the public in this manner; but for that I did not care—I determined to impose upon them too, as soon as I got a chance. Soon after, a school-mate encased me in a remarkably tight pair, during an afternoon's visit; and having, as she said, 'made me look quite genteel,' I departed for home with the delightful consciousness of being 'something of a figure.' Before bed-time I had a romp in the garden with my wild brother and Charles Tracy; I experienced a feeling of suffocation, while running through the paths, that became quite insupportable.

"Why Amy!" exclaimed Charles as he grasped my arm, "What *is* the matter? you look quite black in the face!" They all gathered around me, but unable to speak, I sank back into Charles Tracy's arms, and lost all consciousness.

When I recovered, I found myself lying on my own little bed, with my mother bending fondly over me—the cause of all this trouble on a chair at my side—and Mammy, dear, good Mammy! regarding me with a puzzled look of surprise.

"Why, she actually fainted!" whispered Jane, "just dead away, like any grown person!"

"No," replied Mammy, "the child was dreadfully squeezed, and that took away her breath. She'll kill herself next, with some of her capers!"

Mamma now made a sign for them to be quiet, and stooping down close to my face, asked me how I felt. I tried to answer, "better;" but the words almost choked me, and I still experienced a difficulty in breathing. The evil consequences of this attempt at the graceful were but temporary, however; and the next morning, as I sat up quite recovered, a discussion took place between mamma and the old nurse on the propriety of equipping me at once in corsets to improve my figure. I soon experienced the delight of possessing a pair of my own; on which memorable occasion, I resolved that, like the old woman, I would "neither borrow nor lend;" but the present was conditional—on the first instance of my lacing too tight it was to be taken from me. I took care that this should never happen—that is, to such a degree as to expose myself to punishment; but in many a scene of enjoyment did I suffer the consequences of my foolish vanity. Often while music, and dancing, and everything contributed to render a children's party delightful, I sat apart in a corner, or else went languidly through the figures of the dance, while every nerve throbbed with acute pain.

Ellen and I had for sometime noticed that Charles and Henry were more together than ever. They seldom associated with us now, or asked us to join them; Henry proved faithless with respect to a table he had promised my doll, and Charles refused, for the present, to dig his sister's garden spot; therefore we put our two wise heads together and concluded that this must mean something. The moment school was out, the cap was hastily snatched from its nail in the entry, and they both sallied forth together—where, or for what purpose, we tried in vain to discover. On Saturdays they were constantly at work in the barn, hammering, and cutting, and shaving; and one day we detected them making, over a fire which they had built on bricks in the open air, something which smelt very much like molasses candy. But upon Ellen's venturing to communicate this to Charles, he answered contemptuously that "it was just like girls!—always fancying that everything was something eatable!"

The two made a journey to town together, and came back

Ella Rodman

laden with sundry parcels; and notwithstanding all this business, Henry found time to be very industrious in weeding the flower-beds, for which my father paid him so much an hour—and I noticed that he was uncommonly punctual in presenting his bills. Without being very penetrating, we discovered that the scheme, whatever it might be, was one that required a great deal of time, a great deal of shopping, and a great deal of money. We racked our brains in vain, and not a single mite of information could we extract from the boys; indeed, we might just as well have attacked two pine boards, for they pretended to be deaf as soon as we commenced our inquiries. Ellen began to be afraid that they meditated living on some wild island, like Robinson Crusoe, for she had seen Charles privately appropriate a hatchet, and a ball of twine; and I inclined to the opinion that they were both going to sea, and represented to Ellen how delightful it would be to have them making voyages and bringing us shells, and corals, and all sorts of curious things. But I was the greatest philosopher of the two, for my more timid playmate cried bitterly at the idea; and it was sometime before I could succeed in pacifying her.

We one day discovered the boys in an old barn on the premises; and waiting patiently near by until we saw them depart on some errand to the house, we perceived, to our great joy that the door was unfastened; and effecting a hasty entrance, we expected to be almost as well rewarded for our trouble as was Blue-beard's wife on entering the forbidden chamber. But nothing could we see except a few old boxes turned upside down, and along one side a neat row of shelves. We perceived indeed that the small window now contained four panes of glass, and we also discovered two or three little shelves there. But here our discoveries ended; there was nothing to account for all the labor and privacy that had been going on for the last two or three weeks,—and quite in despair, we returned to the house before the boys discovered our prying.

Things continued in this state for sometime longer; and finding that all our efforts at discovery were not rewarded with the slightest success, we assumed an appearance of proud indifference, and pretended to be as much occupied with our dolls and baby-houses as they were with their barn. Now and then one of the boys, in the tantalizing spirit of mischief, would thrust a parcel under our very eyes, exclaiming at the same time: "Wouldn't you like to see the inside, though? Confess, now, that you would give your very ears to know what's in it!"

"Indeed, and we would not!" in great indignation, "not we! We supposed that it was some boys' nonsense not worth talking about, and were quite occupied with our own affairs, without troubling ourselves about them."

In a tone that sounded very much as though he were in earnest, Charles would continue: "Suppose, Henry, that we let them know what it is, if they promise not to tell—shall we?"

"By no means," Henry would reply, with the air of a Socrates, "Women can never keep a secret—I have heard my father say so."

"We were sure we didn't want to hear their secrets!" and indignantly clipping away with our scissors, we turned a deaf ear to all further remarks. However, the secret did come to light after a while, and in a most unexpected manner.

We had just received a liberal allowance of pocket-money, and while Ellen and I deliberated on the various ways in which it might be spent to advantage, Henry asked us, with a perfectly grave face, if we had heard of the new store lately opened near us? *New* store! Why there had never been any store at all, except the little stand kept by old Betty Tweednor, and now Henry spoke of the new store as though such a thing had ever existed. Certainly we had not heard of it; but resolving to remain no longer in ignorance, we seized our bonnets, and were ready to start in a moment. Henry looked very knowing and mysterious; but following his guidance, we soon found ourselves at the barn which had before excited our curiosity. Why, it had been turned into a regular shop! Rows of candies, better known among children as "barber's-poles," looked imposingly out of the window, and these were flanked by piles of pea-nuts, apples, &c. But all these would have been nothing without that delight of childhood—taffy-candy; and upon a further investigation, we discovered a very ingenious pair of clam-shell scales, with holes bored for strings to pass through, and suspended from a stout stick which was kept in its place by being fastened to an upright piece of wood at each end—the whole resting upon a very complete counter formed of old boxes. It looked exactly like a real store; and behind the counter stood Charles, as demure as possible,—while crowds of our schoolmates gazed, admired, and wondered.

A sign near the door informed passers that "the proprietors, grateful for past favors and the patronage of a liberal public, would continue the business under the firm of Chesbury and Tracy." It would be a somewhat difficult task, we thought, to discover the favors and patronage alluded to; but the young merchants had concluded that this clause gave a dignity and air of reality to the whole. We experienced the pleasure of making purchases, weighed out to us from the much admired clam-shell scales, and were very particular in exacting full weight. Each sale was recorded in a small account book; and long after we had grown to the years of discretion, our mirth was excited by accidentally meeting with this juvenile record. So many purchases were made that afternoon, that the young storekeepers perceived with dismay the very visible decrease in their supplies. We accused them of retrenching considerably in their quantities, on this discovery, and thought that they were too inexperienced for so weighty an office.

Ellen and I often added to their stores by little pies and cakes which we manufactured at home; and in process of time their articles embraced such a variety that the shop became quite celebrated. Even mamma would sometimes come to make purchases; and the boy-merchants found their scheme a very profitable one. But alas! it vanished with the last summer breath; the early snows surrounded their little store, and all access became inconvenient. So they had a sale at prime cost—and we then obtained most wonderful bargains in the confectionary line. Finding himself quite wealthy now, Charles could well afford to be generous; and presented me with a new doll, and his sister Ellen with a miniature set of cups and saucers, over which we had many happy tea-drinkings. We received no presents from Henry, and heard nothing of his money; and it was not till some time after, and then through another source, that we learned that his portion had materially helped to keep a poor woman from freezing during the winter. My father often remarked of Henry, that "he was too generous and self-forgetful ever to be rich;" but there is no doubt that such have their reward—in their own consciences at least.

Ella Rodman

CHAPTER IX

The winter wore rapidly away with sleigh-riding, snow-balling, and our usual parties; and spring, lovely spring! again made its appearance. Our flower-garden looked its very loveliest at this season; for it boasted countless stores of hyacinths, tulips, daffodils, blue-bells, violets, crocuses, &c. I remember so well when we first noticed the little green sprouts shooting up in spots from which the snow had melted; and on making this discovery, we always danced into the house and shouted out: "Spring has come!" It gladdened our very hearts to find the first little violet that dared to show its head above the ground; and then we ran to the peach-trees to look at the delicate pink buds that shot forth so curiously without any leaves. There was a warm sweet breath abroad upon the air that tossed our hair about, and fanned our flushed cheeks, and we knew that it was spring, sweet spring! that had come again to us. Oh, how delightful it was when, escaped from all watchful eyes, I could throw aside the troublesome sun-bonnet, that so obstructed my sight, and dig and delve at pleasure! Never in all my life have I been so happy as in these delightful spring days, when I roved about the paths with a heart full of happiness, and a sensation of thankfulness for the blessings I enjoyed.

Two circumstances contributed materially to immortalize this particular spring in my recollections: I then completed my tenth year, which I thought left me on the very threshold of womanhood, and we had two pet squirrels, who inhabited the locust trees in front of the house, with a tin cage to retire to at night—one of whom we called "blackey," and the other "browney," from their different colors.

"Blackey" was extremely mischievous, and rarely could be caught; but "browney" seemed a perfect paragon of gentleness and goodness—and I would seat myself on the steps, holding him for hours, and listening to the monotonous hum of the locusts, which always filled my heart with a sense of quiet happiness. Did you never sit watching the glorious sunbeams, as they fell on the soft, fresh grass, and with this low, soothing hum in your ears, feel that the earth was very beautiful? I have; but then I was a dreamer—an unmistakable, enthusiastic dreamer, and my fancies would, perhaps, be laughed at by the wise ones of earth.

To return to "browney;" my love cooled for him very suddenly one morning, as, with my finger in close proximity to his mouth, I sat and apostrophized him thus, "You dear, little angel, you! I love you dearly!" a sudden closing of sharp little teeth on my poor fingers put an end to my rhapsodies; and the "little angel" was most unceremoniously dropped on the ground, from whence he made his escape to his usual home, the locust tree—and I never again sought to entice him from his retreat. I ran about the walks as usual this spring, but it was with languor and indifference that I visited our usual haunts; and I wondered what it was that made my steps so very slow and dragging—it seemed as though a weight were tied on each heel. If I attempted a race with the boys, I was obliged to give up from very weariness; and laughing at what they termed my laziness, they pursued their amusements without me. Charles Tracy would now and then bring me a bunch of wild flowers; and to the surprise of all, I preferred sitting with them in my hands to joining in my usual noisy games. I grew pale and thin; and Mammy and

Ella Rodman

Jane began to express their uneasiness about me, while I often noticed my mother's eyes fixed upon me in tender solicitude.

I went to bed one night feeling restless and feverish. It was the latter part of April, and a small wood-fire still burned on the hearth; on the embers of which I fixed my eyes steadfastly, until strange shapes and burning eyes seemed moving about the quiet hearth. I was quite alone; Mammy had gone out to spend the evening, and Jane was taking her tea in the kitchen. Had it been for life or death I could not have spoken; I tried to scream—but a hollow sound rattled in my ears—and with the cold drops gathering on my forehead, I lay still, subdued, in a state of delirious agony. I was almost senseless; until at length, feeling a touch upon my arm, and a breathing at my side, I started wildly up, and eluding all pursuit, fled swiftly down the stair-case. I pressed my hand tightly on my throbbing head, and gaining the kitchen, burst suddenly in, exclaiming, "O! Jane! Jane! do not leave me again!" I sunk down insensible; and remember nothing but a scream of horror which proceeded from Jane, who, having just seated herself beside me as I sprang out of bed, had followed me in a state of breathless alarm to the kitchen.

When I again opened my eyes, it was about midnight. I had been conveyed to my mother's room, and now experienced the delightful sensation of finding myself in a high bed, with curtains; while my head was raised up with pillows to an unusual height. In turning myself to obtain a better view of the surrounding scenery, I became conscious of a stiffness in my right arm; and fairly shuddered with horror on perceiving a basin of blood close to my bedside. But worse and worse! a few paces further off stood a grave-looking man, whom, from his very air, I knew to be a doctor. Nay, had I been at all doubtful on this point, the addition of a pair of spectacles would have convinced me at once—as this is an ornament especially pertaining to M. D.'s. I had always hated, loathed, dreaded a doctor as I would a nauseous object; and I now trembled to find myself in his power—fearing that he read my dislike in my face. Spectacles, too, disconcerted me; the glimmer of the polished glass seems to add new fire to the eyes beneath; and I now beheld a pair, eyes and all, levelled directly upon me. I shuddered at the very idea of a doctor, and could never sit still in the room with one; and now there stood that horrid man, evidently regarding me as his victim, while I felt too weak and sick to make the least resistance.

My aversion probably arose from the circumstance of once having had a loose front tooth pulled out—one that was just ready to jump out itself; which operation, I felt convinced, had left my system in a very shattered state. Often since did I torture myself for hours by mounting up on a table before the glass, and with a string tied around a loosened tooth, give it a little cowardly pull at intervals—lacking sufficient courage to rid myself of my trouble at once. I have sometimes sat in this interesting position for a whole morning; and should probably have continued it through the afternoon had not Fred, or Henry, perceiving my employment, come slyly behind me and caused me to start suddenly, which always dislodged the troublesome tooth.

My eyes rested a moment on the doctor, and then glanced off to seek some more agreeable object, and having found mamma, she seemed like a lovely angel in comparison with the ogre who, I felt convinced, only waited his opportunity to put an end to my life. Mamma came close to me, and observing my gaze still bent upon the basin, she whispered softly: "Do not look so frightened, Amy, you have only been bled—that is all, believe me."

All! After this announcement I wondered that I breathed at all; and had I not been too weak should certainly have cried over the thoughts of the pain I must have suffered in my insensibility. I made no reply, but leaned my head droopingly

Ella Rodman

upon the pillow; and Dr. Irwin, taking my hand, observed: "She is very weak, and we may expect delirium before morning."

His first assertion received the lie direct in the strength with which I pushed him off, as I would the touch of a viper; and clinging to mamma, I cried: "Take him away, dear mother! Take him away!—Do not let him come near us!"

"What?" exclaimed the doctor good-humoredly, "are you afraid of me, my little lady? Do I look so very frightful?"

I was quite surprised at his pleasant tone, and on a nearer survey of his features, felt my passion considerably cooled; but those odious spectacles spoiled all. I remember soon after being raised up, while some one held a cup to my lips, but whether the draught were good or bad I was unable to determine. Dr. Irwin now took my mother aside, and whispered something in a low tone, as he placed a small packet in her hands. I heard my mother say: "I am afraid she will never take it, doctor," to which he replied: "But she *must* take it, madam—we cannot consider a child's humors in the scale with her life." I now felt assured that some nauseous compound was being prepared for me; which I firmly resolved to fling in the doctor's face, should he dare to approach me with it. I was a perfect fury when roused; and this fancied cruelty excited my strongest passions.

But Dr. Irwin wisely took himself off; and the next morning poor mamma received half the mixture on her dress, while the other half found a resting place on the floor—a few drops only having slipped down my throat; while one of the servants heard my screams at the end of the village, and the next door neighbor, prompted by humanity, sent to inquire the name of the murdered party. The next dose was more successful; mamma having spread out before my eyes all her possessions which she thought likely to tempt me, I received permission to make a choice, on condition of swallowing a spoonful of calomel jalap. I further displayed my gentleness by biting Dr. Irwin's fingers when he attempted to look at my throat, and the good man evidently regarded me as a pretty refractory patient.

I always had a great horror of being sick—that is, a real, regular fit of sickness, where you are perched up in bed, and have to do as other people please, and have only just what covering they please—when you are not suffered to put an arm out, or toss off a quilt that almost smothers you, or drink a drop of cold water. Once in a while, I thought, to be just sufficiently sick to sit in the easy chair and look over mother's pretty things, or daub with her color-box, while people brought me oranges and waited upon me, did very well. I was not a gentle, timid, feminine sort of a child, as I have said before—one who would faint at the prick of a pin, or weep showers of tears for a slight headache; I was a complete little hoyden, full of life and spirits, to whom the idea of being in bed in the day-time was extremely disagreeable—and when I had been "awful," according to the nursery phraseology, the greatest punishment that could be inflicted upon me was to send me thither to enjoy the charms of solitude. I was a female edition of my brother Fred; not quite so prone to tricks and mischief, perhaps—but almost as wild and unmanageable.

Now and then Fred would come down in the morning pale, sick, and subdued-looking; his head tightly bound with a handkerchief, and his whole countenance expressive of suffering. A sick headache was the only thing that could tame him; and a smile of ineffable relief sat on the faces of the others as they glanced at his woe-begone visage. He was as secure for that day as though chained hand and foot. My quiet hours were when some fascinating book engrossed my whole attention; I drank in each word, and could neither see nor hear anything around.

Ella Rodman

But here I was, really sick and quiet, ill in bed for a whole month—day-time and all; and oh! the nauseous doses that somehow slipped down my unwilling throat! Sometimes I would lie and watch the others moving around and doing as they chose, and then, feeling galled by my own sense of dependence and inefficiency, the warm blood would glow quickly as before, and springing hastily up, I determined to throw off this weary feeling of lassitude. But it was of no use; all I could do was to sink back exhausted, and "bide my time."

When the first stage of my illness was passed, poor mamma, completely worn out, would often leave me to the care of Mammy or Jane; with numerous directions to see that I took whatever had been left for me by Doctor Irwin. I always liked to have Jane with me, for I *loved* her; and the medicine never seemed to taste so bad when she gave it to me. She had various ways of smoothing this disagreeable duty; and one night when I had been rather obstreperous, she cut a pill in two and took half, by way of keeping me company; saying as she swallowed it that "perhaps it might do her some good." When I became well enough to leave my bed I sat in a nice easy-chair drawn close up to the window, from whence I could see the early flowers that were now blooming in full beauty in the garden below, while some amusing book rested on my lap. I remember that they brought me the very first strawberries that ripened; and the neighbors were so kind that many a well-relished delicacy was sent in "for Mrs. Chesbury's sick child."

I was just able to run about, but still looking very pale and thin, when Aunt Henshaw arrived on a visit. "What!" exclaimed she, "can this be the madcap, Amy? Why, you look like a ghost, child! What in the world have you been doing to yourself—studying too hard?"

The old lady possessed no great powers of penetration, and

not being sufficiently discerning to distinguish between the love of reading and the love of study, she concluded, from seeing me often with a book in my hand, that I was quite a studious character. Aunt Henshaw remained a week or two; and though not exactly sick, I remained thin and drooping, and seemed to get no stronger as the season advanced. The state of my health was canvassed over and over again in the family circle; and one day, when they were all gazing upon me with anxious solicitude, and remarking upon my pale cheeks, Aunt Henshaw observed: "She needs a change of air, poor child! She must go home with me."

Ella Rodman

CHAPTER X

I was quite surprised at the effect which this remark produced. Although an only daughter, I had never been much caressed at home—I was always so troublesome that they loved me best at a distance. If I happened to get into the library with my father, I was sure to upset the inkstand, or shake the table where he sat writing—or if admitted to my mother's apartment, I made sad havoc with her work-basket, and was very apt to clip up cut out articles with my little scissors—which said scissors I regarded with the greatest affection; in the first place because they were my own private property, and in the next place, they afforded me the delightful pleasure of clipping—that great enjoyment of childhood; but they did so much mischief that complaints against them were loud and long, and I quite trembled at an oft-repeated threat of taking them away.

My mother evidently disapproved of Aunt Henshaw's proposal, and my father drawing me towards him affection-ately, said: "I am afraid we could not part with our little madcap—we should miss her noise sadly."

The idea of being missed, and actually made a subject of argument, was something quite new to me; and glancing in surprise from one to the other, I awaited the issue in silence, scarcely knowing whether I wished to go or stay. But Aunt Henshaw carried her point. She represented so many advantages to be gained by the change, where I could run about quite wild, rolling among the fresh hay, and breathing the pure air—insisting that it must bring a color into my pale cheeks—that my parents at length yielded.

Now began the delightful bustle of preparation. My mother turned over my scanty wardrobe with perplexed looks; and an immediate cutting and clipping took place, by which old gowns of hers were made into bran new ones for me. Nor was this all—some were bought on purpose for me; and I had two or three delightful jaunts to the city, to choose the patterns for myself; and I wondered if anybody ever had so many, new things at once as I was about to have. I became quite a wonder in the family—a person whose movements were of the utmost importance; for I was going to be away from them the whole summer, and it seemed an almost endless separation. Mammy was not at all pleased at their sending her child away from her; the old nurse even cried over me, and insisted upon it that I had always been a paragon of excellence, and that she could not live without me. My father gave me some money to buy her a present, the selection of which was to be left entirely to my own taste; and the sum I expended in a manner perfectly characteristic: I procured a large bunch of gay beads for Mammy, and presented Jane with the wonderful history of little Red Riding Hood. Both treasured them as carefully, and apparently valued them as highly, as if they had been better selected; and being quite confident that they would prefer them to anything else, I was much surprised at the disapprobation expressed in the family circle.

I gave Henry a little pincushion, which I made on purpose for him, and not knowing what to present Fred with, I allowed him to rip open my second-best doll, which was still in quite a good state of preservation. Fred had always possessed an inquiring mind, and an inclination to inspect the contents of everything, in consequence of which my possessions often suffered—and this employment now afforded him the most intense satisfaction; while I, with a certain feeling of curiosity, and yet scarcely able to repress an effort for the rescue of poor dolly, stood watching the proceeding. Nothing appeared, however, but saw-dust; although Fred had positively assured me that he had no doubt we would find a diamond ring, or a piece of money, at least—as people often did where they least expected it; and it was partly this consideration that led me to consent to the dissection, for we had made an agreement to divide the spoils.

Fred's head was always filled with wonderful schemes of this nature, and if he had not been so lazy and fond of mischief he would have made a smart boy; for he was always reading books containing wonderful researches into the productions of former centuries; and being particularly interested in the study of minerals and different species of rock, he often endeavored to explain to me the various forms of strata which were found below the earth; but my comprehension could not take it in. He was continually poring over fossil remains, and digging in the garden for something curious. He one day ran in with his apron full of stones and other rubbish, and holding up in triumph an object of various hues, through which a slight blue shade was distinctly visible, he called out eagerly: "See, mother! I have really found some fossil remains at last!"

Mamma took the admired treasure in her hand, as Fred desired; and as she did so, a smile that had hovered about her mouth grew deeper and deeper; and finally her amusement burst forth in a hearty laugh. Fred seized his prize indignantly, and after washing it with the greatest care, found himself in possession of the spout of an old crockery tea-pot. We heard no more of fossil remains after that; though he still pursued his researches privately—having, I believe transferred his expectations from fossil remains to golden treasures. He was hardly more successful in this line, as he never found anything to reward his toil except a solitary five-pence, that he mistook for a gold piece, and which required more rubbing and scouring to make it distinguishable than it was worth. Having sacrificed my doll on the shrine of sisterly affection, not to mention the dross of private interest, I concluded that I had done as much for Fred as he had any right to expect; and employed myself in arranging sugar-plums in various attractive forms, as farewell presents to my younger brothers.

The eventful morning arrived on which I was to take my departure. It was my first absence from home for any length of time, and I had scarcely been able to sleep at all during the night—my mind being occupied with the one all-engrossing thought. I scarcely dared to listen at first, for fear I should hear it rain; but the sun shone brightly in all the glory of a clear June morning, and springing out of bed, I dressed myself as expeditiously as possible, for fear that Aunt Henshaw might go off without me. "What then was my surprise, when after breakfast I saw the old lady sit down as usual, and after carefully wiping her spectacles, take up a book she had been perusing, just as if the greatest event of my life were not about to occur that very day?

"Why, Aunt Henshaw!" said I in a tone of acute disappointment, "Are we not going to-day?"

"Certainly, my dear," was her reply, "But the stage coach will not be here till two o'clock, and I have all my things ready."

What could I possibly do with the six intervening hours? I too had all my things ready; and my spirits were now in a state that absolutely required excitement of some kind or other. I tried to read, but it was impossible to fix my thoughts on the subject—even the Arabian Nights failed to interest

Ella Rodman

me; and after wondering for some time at Aunt Henshaw, who could view the near prospect of a journey that would occupy two or three days with the most perfect composure, I proceeded to my mother's apartment. I had not been there long before I got up a cry, and felt more doubtful than ever whether I wished to go. But mamma talked with me for some time; and having clearly ascertained that it was my parents' wish that I should go, in hopes of benefiting my health by the change, I comforted myself with the idea of martyrdom on a small scale.

I put my doll to board with Ellen Tracy until my return, at a charge of so many sugar-plums a week; with strict injunctions not to pull its arms or legs out of order, or attempt to curl its hair. I could not eat a mouthful of dinner, but Aunt Henshaw stowed away some cake for me in a corner of her capacious bag; a proceeding which then rather amused me, but for which I was afterwards exceedingly thankful. The time seemed almost interminable; I threw out various hints on the value of expedition, the misery of being behindhand, and the doubtful punctuality of stage-coaches—but Aunt Henshaw remained immovable.

"As to its coming before the appointed time," said she, "I never heard of such a thing. It is much more likely to leave us altogether."

Dreadful idea! Suppose it should! I stood flattening my nose against the window-pane in hopes of spying the welcome vehicle; but it did not even glimmer in the far distance. Full half an hour before the time, I was equipped in the wrappers which my invalid state required, impatiently awaiting the expected clatter of wheels. At length it rolled rapidly up to the door; a shabby-looking vehicle, drawn by four horses—and a perfect wilderness of heads and eyes looked forth from the windows, while legs and arms dangled from the top. It was quite full; and several voices called out, "They can't come in, driver! It's impossible!"

What a blank fell upon my hopes at these cruel words! The people looked so savage and unpitying, and I thought that after all we must stay at home—there seemed no crevice of space into which we could force ourselves; and in silent consternation I surveyed Aunt Henshaw's substantial proportions. But she was an experienced traveller; and making her adieus with a degree of composure and certainty that quite reassured me, she took me by the hand and advanced to the stage as smilingly as though they had all invited her to enter. The driver's eagle eye spied out a seat for Aunt Henshaw—a kind-looking old gentleman took me on his lap—the door was closed, and away we rattled. Aunt Henshaw, never much given to silence, found a congenial companion in the gentleman who had given me a seat; they were soon engaged in an animated conversation on the pleasures of farming, during which I went to sleep—nor was I aroused until about two hours after, when we found ourselves landed at the wharf. We went on board the packet, and proceeded to the cabin, where I was surprised, amused, and rather frightened at the appearance of the narrow-looking boxes which we were destined to sleep in. But Aunt Henshaw assured me that there was no danger; and I found from experience that I could sleep almost as well there as in my own bed at home.

The wind was unfavorable, and we were almost a week on the water; but at length we reached New London and proceeded to Waterford. Aunt Henshaw's family, I knew, consisted only of a daughter—her sons having married and settled away from her—and to the meeting with this cousin Statia, I looked forward with some anxiety. It was almost dark when we approached the house; a real farmhouse, with lilac and syringa bushes in front, and a honeysuckle running over the piazza. A little dog came out and barked at us—a sensible-looking cat rested on the porch—and in the doorway stood Cousin Statia. She kissed me affectionately, and appeared glad to see her mother; and we were all soon seated around the table, where fresh cottage-cheese, crimson radishes, and warm tea-cakes looked invitingly forth.

I was rather disappointed in the appearance of Cousin Statia; I had expected to see a fresh, smiling-looking country girl, but I found a stiff, demure-looking young lady, at whose age I scarcely dared venture a guess. A little colored girl waited on the table, who evidently surveyed me with a great deal of interest; for I constantly caught the sharp glances of her little black eyes. She had been christened Aholibama—a name which she told me was taken out of some story-book, though I afterwards found that it was in the Bible—but this being too long an appellation, they had abbreviated it to Holly. During a hasty glance into the cheerful kitchen, I caught a glimpse of a very nice-looking colored woman, who, I afterwards found, was Sylvia, the cook.

Everything looked very pleasant around, though plain; but I was tired and sleepy, and at an early hour Cousin Statia conducted me to a small, neat room in the second story, with white curtains; and after ascertaining that I could undress myself, she left me for a short time, promising to come and take the candle. I felt the least bit homesick and wished very much to see them all; but I was also very much interested in the novelty of a new scene, and anticipated a great deal of pleasure in examining the premises. Aunt Henshaw had told me that she believed there were kittens somewhere around, and I determined to search till I found them; for a little pet kitten appeared to me the sweetest of all created things.

In the meantime, I began to experience a very uncomfortable sensation that quickly swallowed up all other thoughts. Cousin Statia had taken the candle, but it was a bright, moonlight night, and the beautiful moonbeams that came dancing in and formed a perfect network upon the floor, made the room almost as light as day. It was not very warm weather, but I felt the perspiration pouring down, while I trembled in every limb. My eyes were fixed with a sort of fascination on the opposite wall, where the shadow of a figure seemed to pass and repass; and every time it arrived at a certain point, there was a sort of a kick up, as though with the feet behind. I looked all around, as soon as I dared to, but everything was still except the tormenting shadow. I scarcely breathed, but kept watching the queer figure, till I was almost ready to faint from cowardice. I tried to reason with myself—and called to mind how my father had endeavored to banish this weakness; how one night on being afraid to go into the cellar, he had himself gone with me and examined every corner, to convince me that there was nothing to fear; and under the impulse of these reflections I sprang out of bed, determined to investigate the mystery. I went in every part of the room; I examined the window, the curtains, but nothing was to be seen, while the figure still continued its movements; and almost sick, I returned to bed, to lie and watch the shadow. All sorts of queer stories rushed into my head; I tried to forgot them and think of something else, but it was impossible. The movement was slow, regular, and punctual.

At last I could stand it no longer; I rushed to the window, determined to stay there till the mystery was explained, for I felt convinced that I should find it there. I directed my eyes piercingly to every part of the curtains; and at length I perceived that the window had been let down at the top. I closed it, arranged the curtains differently, and then, in some trepidation, returned to my shadow. It had disappeared; and I now understood that the formidable figure was merely a part of the curtain, which, influenced by the night wind, swayed to and fro, causing the shadow on the wall.

I do not think I ever experienced a cowardly feeling afterwards; that night perfectly satisfied me that superstition was the most unreasonable torture that could be inflicted on

Ella Rodman

oneself; and I was ever afterwards celebrated for my bravery. Even my father praised my conduct, and said that it was pretty well for a girl of ten years, under such circumstances —at the same time representing to me how much more reasonable such a course was, than screaming would have been, to rouse the household for nothing. I went quietly to sleep, and dreamed neither of goblins nor ghosts, but of a dear little spotted kitten with a blue ribbon around its neck.

CHAPTER XI

I did not wake very early the next morning, and when I opened my eyes, I perceived Cousin Statia standing by my bedside, who had been endeavoring to waken me. Her manner was rather solemn as she announced that Aunt Henshaw was waiting for me to commence the morning services. At this information I felt very much mortified; and springing quickly out of bed, I was soon dressed and in the breakfast room. Aunt Henshaw sat with a large Bible open before her; and after kissing me kindly, she read a chapter, and then offered a short prayer.

After breakfast, Cousin Statia proceeded to wash up the cups and saucers, which she always did for fear of their being broken; Aunt Henshaw proceeded to the poultry yard, and I accompanied her. She had a large tin pan in her hand, filled with moistened Indian meal, with which she fed the chickens; of which there seemed an endless number, both old and young. Then we went to the barn-yard, and she showed me a young calf; but it was an awkward-looking thing, that scampered about without sense or meaning. But I had not forgotten the kittens, and I asked Aunt Henshaw where they were. She said that she would look; and going into the barn, we peered around, in mangers and out-of-the-way places, without the least success; and we concluded that the old cat must have hid them up in the mow.

Ella Rodman

"Perhaps Holly knows, though," said the old lady, on noticing my disappointment, "very little escapes her eyes, and we can at least call her and see."

Holly was called, but with not much more success than our hunt after the kittens, so we were obliged to proceed to the kitchen—a wing on the same floor with the parlor and dining-room. Holly was now visible, peeling apples, and evidently glad to be released from her task, she professed herself perfectly acquainted with the whereabouts of the kittens.

"But can we get them?" asked Aunt Henshaw.

"Oh yes, Missus," replied Holly, "if you'll only 'tice the old cat somewhere and shut her up. She'd 'spect suthin' if she saw me, and there'd be no gittin' rid of her; and if she once ketched us at the bisness, she'd scratch our very eyes out—cats is always dreadful skeery about their kittens."

There was something in this speech which grated on my ear as painfully ungrammatical; and I resolved, on the first opportunity, to instruct Holly in the rudiments of grammar. She remained in the kitchen while Aunt Henshaw, after calling "pussy" in an affectionate manner, shut the cat up in the dining-room; and our guide then led the way to the kittens. The garret stairs turned off in two directions; one led to about four or five steps, beneath which was a hollow place extending some distance back, where Holly had often seen the old cat go in and out in a private manner.

"Now," said she, "you stay here, and I'll jest git the rake and rake the kittens out for Miss Amy, here."

"But I am afraid you will hurt them," said Aunt Henshaw.

"It ain't very likely," replied Holly confidently, "that they're a-going to be so shaller as to git hurt. They'll squirm over the points of the rake, and take care of themselves."

The rake was brought; and five little sprawling kittens, with their eyes scarcely open, were soon crawling at my feet. "Oh, you dear little angels!" I exclaimed in ecstasy.

"Rather black-looking angels," said Aunt Henshaw with a smile.

I took them up, one after another, and was quite at a loss which to admire most. There were three black ones, one grey, and one white one spotted. I rather thought I preferred the white and grey, while Holly claimed the three black ones. We took them all to the kitchen and placed a saucer of milk before them, while Holly let out the cat, that she might see how well we were treating them. She looked around in surprise at first; but then deliberately taking them one by one, she carried them all off in her mouth, and we saw nothing more of them for some time.

I spent the morning in wandering about; and in the afternoon I sat in the parlor with Cousin Statia, who was knitting as fast as her needles could fly. I asked her for a book; and after some search, she handed me the "Pilgrim's Progress," in which I soon became deeply interested, while Aunt Henshaw took a nap in her chair. Towards evening the old white horse was harnessed up, and we took a drive; Aunt Henshaw being determined, as she said, to put some color in my pale cheeks. They evidently thought a great deal of this old horse, whom they called Joe; but I mentally compared him with my father's carriage-horses—a comparison not much to his advantage. Cousin Statia drove, but Joe did not seem much disposed to go. Every now and then he came to a stand-still, and I quite wanted to get out and push him along. But they saw nothing uncommon in his behavior, and even congratu-lated themselves upon his being so careful. Aunt Henshaw

Ella Rodman

said that such dreadful accidents had happened in conesquence of horses running away with people, and that Joe's great virtue consisted in his being so perfectly gentle.

We did not drive very far, and on our return found that Sylvia had tea all ready and waiting for us. The old colored woman was quite tasty in her ideas, and had garnished an immense dish of strawberries with flowers and leaves, through which the red fruit gleamed most temptingly forth. After tea, when Cousin Statia had taken up her knitting, and Aunt Henshaw was seated in her usual chair, I placed a low stool beside her for myself, and begged for one of her usual stories. She was a very entertaining old lady, with a great deal of natural wit, and abundant reminiscences of the times in which she had lived. Nothing delighted us more than to hear her stories of the Revolution, in many of which she figured as principal actor; and I now expected a rich treat.

"Well, I do not know," replied Aunt Henshaw in answer to my question, "I think I must have told you all."

This remark, I knew from experience, was the prelude to something even more interesting than usual, and I waited patiently for her to begin.

"Did I ever tell you," she continued, "of the time that Statia went to her Uncle Ben's at night, with no one except her two little brothers?"

I had never heard the narrative, and eagerly settled myself in the position of a listener.

"Statia," said her mother, "you had better tell the story— perhaps you remember it better than I do."

"It was a raw November night," she began, "and though it did not exactly storm, the wind moaned and raged through the trees, blowing the fallen leaver about in gusts, and making a pleasant fire seem doubly cheerful. The large hickory logs were roaring and blazing in our huge fireplace and my father, my mother, my two brothers, and myself were gathered around the fire. I was the eldest, but I was then only twelve years old; and yet, I remember always to have felt a great deal of care and responsibility towards the other children I never can forget the night, for I then experienced my first lesson of self-forgetfulness; and whenever I speak of it, it seems as of something just passed. As I was saying, we all sat by the fire, and had just been talking of the British, who were dreaded and feared by us children as a race of ogres. The door opened suddenly, and John, one of the hired men, stood before us, his countenance expressive of some disaster. My father and mother both rose in apprehension, and demanded the cause of his seeming terror.

"Why sir," he stammered, "perhaps it ain't after all, anything so very bad—there may not be any real danger; though it ain't exactly what you would have chosen. I have just come from the post-office, and they say that a party of British have landed about four miles below, and will probably come and take supper with you. I do not believe they will do anything worse, but it is best to be ready."

My mother turned very pale, but she did not faint; she was a true daughter of America, and always tried to repress all outward signs of weakness. "I can load the guns," said she, "and attend to the supper—but what will become of the children? These soldiers may perhaps be intoxicated, and might set fire to the house."

"They must be sent away," replied my father; "How long will it be before the British get here?" he continued.

"About two hours I should think," was John's reply; "and this being the first farmhouse they pass, they will probably stop here."

"Statia," said my father, turning to me, "it is my wish that you take your brothers and go as quickly as possible to your Uncle Ben's, where you will be out of danger. I must send you *alone*, my child, for I can spare no one to accompany you. But it is not a dark night, and you are well acquainted with the road. I see no other alternative."

"I trembled in every limb, but I had been brought up with the greatest deference for my parents' wishes, and should not have dared to dispute my father's command, even had he told me to do a much harder thing. The children began to cry, for they were afraid of being murdered on the road; but my mother succeeded in soothing them; and well bundled up, we received a kiss and blessing from our parents, and started on our dreary journey. Here was I quite alone, except my two little brothers, who clung to me as we went along, and cried with terror, with three long miles before me, and the wind blowing around us with such fury that we could scarcely keep our feet. My younger brother now complained of the cold; and resolved to protect them at whatever cost to myself, I took off my cloak and wrapped it about him. I had only a shawl left; and wrapping my arms in its thin folds, while the children grasped my skirt, we proceeded slowly along. It was fortunate for us that the moon shone brightly, for, even as it was, I was puzzled about the way. But at length we reached the well-known house, and surprised enough were they to see us; but when we told them the reason, my uncle immediately started for my father's house, to render any assistance that might be required. The night passed, however, without the expected invasion; the British proceeded in another direction, and our cold, lonely walk might have been dispensed with. But my father called me his brave little girl, and said that in future he could always trust me—while my mother pressed us silently to her bosom, and as she kissed us, I felt the warm tears falling on my face. She too had had her trial on that fearful night."

I felt very thankful that my parents had never required such a disagreeable proof of obedience; for, not possessing the firm principle of right which characterized Cousin Statia, even as a child, I should have been very much disposed to resist their authority.

"Well," said Aunt Henshaw, "that is a story of which Statia may well be proud, but her telling it has just put me in mind of something else. I once had a large jar of sour milk standing before the fire, which I was going to make into cottage-cheese, when one of the servants came running, in breathless haste, with the news that three British soldiers were approaching the house. Plunder was generally the object of such stragglers, and there was quite a large sum of gold lying in a bureau drawer, which I felt very unwilling to part with. My husband was from home, so seizing the money, I quietly dropped it all in the jar of milk. I had just finished this exploit when the soldiers entered; and after eating in a manner that made the children fear they would next be precipitated down their capacious throats, they began to look about for plunder. I tried to be as composed as possible, and this, I think, kept them a little in awe; for they were perfectly civil in words, and did no damage, except to turn things topsy turvy. They found nothing to suit them, till spying a very good coat of Mr. Henshaw's, one of them coolly encased himself in it and they all walked off together." I watched them from the window, and perceiving that they had left the gate open, I called out after them: "Be kind enough to shut the gate, will you? I am afraid the pigs will get in." They stopped a moment, smiled, and then did as I requested. "Ah, Amy," said my aunt in conclusion, "the necessity of the times was a school that taught women far more of the realities of life than they learn now-a-days."

Aunt Henshaw fell into a long revery; and a pair of eyes,

which had been glimmering near the door for some time, suddenly disappeared, and I heard the retreating footsteps of Holly as she took her way to the kitchen. The little colored girl always kept her eyes and ears open, and never lost an opportunity to gain knowledge of any description. A great deal which she had stealthily learned was communicated to me during my stay; and I am sorry to say that I was more hurt than benefitted by the companionship. Aunt Henshaw, though kind, did not appear to me in the light of a playmate, and Cousin Statia seldom opened her lips—being too industrious to waste time in talking; so that, for want of more suitable company, I descended to the kitchen.

The next morning, having obtained Aunt Henshaw's permission, I went out to feed the chickens; and having drawn them near the wood-pile, I confined my favors almost exclusively to a sober-looking hen and five little chickens. When the pan was empty, I conceived that I had well earned the right, and putting my hand down softly, I took up a cunning little thing and hugged it in delight. But a terrible flapping of wings sounded close to my ears—I could scarcely distinguish any thing—and dropping the chicken, I fell across the chopping-log. The old hen rushed furiously at me, and kept beating me with her wings; while I, afraid that my eyes would be pecked out, could do nothing but scream. Some one, at length, picked me up; and when I ventured to look around, I beheld Sylvia, who stood beside me, laughing immoderately. Holly soon joined the company, and even Cousin Statia seemed amused; while Aunt Henshaw carefully examined my eyes to see that they had sustained no injury.

"I ought to have told you not to touch the chickens," said the old lady; "for the hen would even sacrifice her life to protect them."

But experience is the best teacher, after all—the lessons thus gained, though more disagreeable, are seldom forgotten; and

I never again meddled with the chickens.

This seemed destined, though, to be a day of misfortunes, to which the chicken business was but a slight commencement. The evening was most lovely, and I accompanied Holly, who bad gone to feed the pigs. A fence separated the pen from the rest of the yard; and on this fence it was Holly's usual practice to perch herself and watch the motions of her charges. She looked so comfortable that I determined to follow her example; and having gained the eminence, I looked around in triumph. But oh, how sad to tell! but a few moments elapsed ere I found myself floundering in the mire beneath; while the pigs all rushed towards me as though I had been thrown there for them to make a supper of. Holly was quite convulsed with laughter; but my screams now became terrific; and calling Sylvia, the two extricated me from my unpleasant predicament.

I was truly a pitiable object, but my white dress was the greatest sufferer: while the tears that rolled down my cheeks grew blacker and blacker as they descended. I almost wished myself home again; but Sylvia, between her paroxyms of laughter, told me "not to cry, and they would soon make me look as good as new—any how, missus musn't see me in such a pickle." They fell to scraping and scouring with the greatest zeal, and then placed me before the kitchen fire to dry.

"How the pigs did run!" said Holly; "'spect, Miss Amy, they mistook you for a little broder!"

At this sally Sylvia laughed louder than ever; but perceiving my distress, she observed, in a kind tone: "Never mind, Miss Amy, we can't help laughing, you know—and you'll laugh too, when you git out of this here mess. But we do really feel sorry for you, for you look reel awful; I only hope old missus won't come in and ketch you."

But in a few moments the kind face of Aunt Henshaw looked into the scene of distress which the kitchen had now become, and surprise at my appearance rendered her almost speechless. But she soon recovered herself; and under her direction I was immersed in a tub of water, while my unfortunate clothes were consigned to the same fate. After this ceremony I was advised to go to bed; and thither I accordingly repaired, thinking how forlorn it was to fall into the pig-pen on such a beautiful evening.

The whole household seemed disposed to bear in mind that unfortunate occurrence; when about to fall into mischief, Aunt Henshaw would say in a peculiar tone: "Remember the pig-pen, Amy!" or, when troubling Sylvia, it would be; "I guess you learned that in the pig-pen, Miss Amy;" and even Holly took up the burden of the song, till I heartily wished that she had taken the plunge instead of myself. Before long they all discovered that I was very prone to such scrapes; I dropped a very nice hat down the well, which, for fear of its spoiling the water, they spent a great deal of time in fishing up—I fell from the mow, but fortunately sustained no injury; and Sylvia one day caught me skimming off the cream—an amusement which I considered very innocent, but she speedily undeceived me.

CHAPTER XII

Two or three weeks passed on very pleasantly, and I began to think it time to write a letter home. I had made but little progress in the art, and letter-writing always appeared to me a great undertaking; but Aunt Henshaw, having one afternoon provided me with pen, ink, and paper, and elevated me nicely with the large Bible and my "Pilgrim's Progress," I sat biting the end of my quill, and pondering over some form of commencement. I had already written "dear mother" at the top; at length I added after considerable reflection:

"I am well, and hope that you are the same. It is very pleasant here. No more at present from

Your affectionate Daughter,

AMY."

Aunt Henshaw pronounced this "very well—what was of it;" and Cousin Statia smiled, though I could not well why; but her smiles were so few and far between that they always set me a wondering. The letter was sealed, however, and enclosed in a larger one of Aunt Henshaw's, who probably gave a more detailed account of matters and things than I had given.

In the meantime, I was fast regaining the blooming, hoyden

Ella Rodman

appearance most natural to me; and Aunt Henshaw continued to write glowing accounts of my improvement. In due time my scrawl was answered by a most affectionate letter from mamma, to which was added a postscript by my father; and I began to rise wonderfully in my own estimation, in consequence of having letters addressed entirely to myself. I even undertook to correct Sylvia for speaking ungrammatically, which made her very angry; and she took occasion to observe, that she had not lived so long in the world to be taught grammar by young ladies who fell into pig-pens. One great source of amusement at Henshaw's, was to watch Sylvia making cheeses. Sometimes she allowed me to make small ones, which I pressed with geranium leaves; but one day, being a little out of humor, she refused to let me have the rennet unless I could find it.—I searched through the kitchen and everywhere for it, and spent the whole morning in looking, till I almost despaired of finding it; but at length I pushed aside a tub, and there it was. This was one of Sylvia's peculiarities. She was an excellent servant, and having been a long time in the family, Aunt Henshaw allowed her to have pretty much her own way. Sylvia was not wanting in sense, and often, when the old lady thought she had obtained the better of the dispute, she was, in reality, yielding to the sagacity of the colored woman. Holly was a sort of satellite, and evidently quite in awe of her superior; but Sylvia regarded her as the very quintescence of laziness, and always delighted to set her at some interminable job. It was much more to Holly's taste to look after the cows and pigs, and wander about the premises, than to wash dishes and peel potatoes; but she dared not resist the cook's authority.

One Sunday morning I was left at home, in consequence of not being well, with strict injunctions not to get into mischief; while Aunt Henshaw, Cousin Statia, and Sylvia went to church—the superintendence of the house being placed in Holly's charge. I settled myself by the parlor window with my "Pilgrim's Progress" and pursued the thread of Christian's adventures; while I glanced from time to time on the prospect without, while the hum of the locusts and lowing of the cows came borne upon my ear like pleasant sounds. I laid down my book to read a chapter in the Bible, and was enjoying a very pleasant frame of mind when the tempter came, in the shape of Holly, and beckoned me into the kitchen.

Nothing loath, I followed eagerly; and the colored girl proposed that we should have a small baking. The fire had been carefully put out in the kitchen, and we concluded to make one on bricks in the yard. After puffing and blowing with considerable energy, Holly kindled a flame; and we then concluded to mix up some gingerbread, and bake it in clam-shells As I heard the monotonous hum of the bees, and remarked the stillness around, while everything seemed to speak of the Sabbath, my conscience reproached me; and I was several times on the point of turning back into the parlor, but I lacked sufficient courage to resist Holly's glowing descriptions of our gingerbread that was to be. The store-room closet was pretty dark, and Holly was obliged to go by guess-work in selecting her materials, but all seemed right; and in triumph we placed several clam-shells of dough on the fire to bake. We worked very hard to keep up the flames, but the baking progressed slowly; and we dreaded to hear the sound of wheels that announced the return of the church-goers. It was done at last, and we sat down to enjoy the feast. I broke off a piece, and put it in my mouth, expecting to find a delicious morsel, but it had a very queer taste; and I saw that Holly was surveying it with an appearance of the greatest curiosity.

"What is the matter?" said I, "What have you done to it, Holly?"

"Well, I guess I've put in lime instead of flour," she replied.

Ella Rodman

It was but too true; and just then we heard the sound of wheels, and a vigorous lifting of the great brass knocker. Holly hurriedly cleared away all signs of our employment, and then opened the door; while I returned to my books, convinced that the poorest time to make gingerbread was on Sunday, and in the dark. But Aunt Henshaw discovered our proceedings through Sylvia, who complained that some one had dropped molasses in the lime; which she soon traced to Holly, and I was never left home again on Sunday, alone.

"Once," said Aunt Henshaw, when I had, as usual, solicited a story, "there was a report that the British were about to sack New London. The city was a scene of hurry and confusion. Carriages were driving hither and thither, laden with silver plate and other valuables, which the owners were glad to place in the hands of any respectable-looking stranger they met, for safe-keeping. Several pieces were placed in our carriage; among others a handsome silver tankard and half-a-dozen goblets, which were never reclaimed. I have always kept them to this day."

She showed me these articles, which were extremely rich and massive, and the old lady always kept them carefully locked in a capacious side-board; never taking them out except to look at.

"Aunt Henshaw, did you ever see a lord?" I inquired.

"Plenty of them," was her reply, "lords were as thick as blackberries during the Revolution."

"How did they look?" said I.

"Very much like other people—and often pretty distressed."

I was then surprised at this information, but I have since learned better; for I have seen the House of Lords in

England, and they are, for the most part, a common, uninteresting-looking assembly.

"There was a Lord Spencer," continued my aunt, "a very wild young man, who was constantly committing some prank or other—though always strictly honorable in repairing any damages he occasioned. He once, for mere sport, shot a fine colt, belonging to an old farmer, as he was quietly grazing in the field. Even his companions remonstrated with him, and endeavored to prevent the mischief; but he laid them a wager that he should not only escape punishment, but that he would even make the old farmer perfectly satisfied with his conduct. They accepted his bet, and anxious to see how he would extricate himself, they accompanied him to the residence of the old farmer.

"That is a very fine colt of yours," began the young lord, "I should like to purchase him."

"He is not for sale," replied the farmer, shortly.

"I suppose not," rejoined the visitor. "But what would you value him at in case any accident happened to him through the carelessness of others? What sum would pay you for it?"

"A hundred dollars would cover his value," said the farmer, after some consideration, "but has any thing happened to him, that you ask these questions?"

"Yes," replied the lord, "I have unfortunately shot him—and here is two hundred dollars as an equivalent."

Lord Spencer won his wager, for the farmer had made at least a hundred dollars, and being extremely fond of money, he could not regret the loss of his colt. "This is a specimen, Amy, of what lords are; so do not go to forming any exalted notions of them, as of a superior race of beings. It was very

Ella Rodman

cruel in Lord Spencer to shoot the poor animal—but it was honorable in him to make up the farmer's loss, for it doubled the amount of wages he gained; yet to sum up the proceeding, it was wrong—for besides killing an inoffensive animal, it did not belong to him."

Aunt Henshaw seldom failed to point out the right and wrong in her stories, for she feared that I would be carried away with whatever was most dazzling, and thus form erroneous impressions. It is an excellent maxim that "people should be just before they are generous;" and did all bear this in mind while admiring actions that often dazzle with a false glitter, they would assume a totally different appearance.

Every few days there was an inundation of different cousins who lived but a few miles distant; and then there was so much shaking of great rough hands, as I was presented—so many comments on my appearance, and comparison of each separate feature with each of my parents—that I grew almost afraid to look up under the many eyes that were bent upon me to detect resemblances to the Henshaws, Chesburys, or Farringtons—which last was my mother's maiden name. I became quite tired of telling people when I arrived, how long I intended to stay, and how many brothers and sisters I had. They were all very kind, though, and invited me so politely to come and see them that I quite wanted to go; and Aunt Henshaw promised to return their visits very soon, and bring me with her.

So one fine day we set forth on a visit to Cousin Ben's—a son of the identical Uncle Ben to whose house Cousin Statia walked with her two little brothers, on that cold November night. She pointed out the road as we passed, showed me the very place where she had wrapped her own cloak around her brother, the spot where they stopped to rub their hands warm, and a cross-road which they came very near taking. The house was plain, but pleasantly situated; and as we drove up to the door, Cousin Ben, his wife, and two or three children about my own age, came out to meet us. There was very little reserve among these country cousins; and before long, I was on as good terms with my play-mates as though I had known them all my life. We raced out into the fields, and feasted on sugar-pears, which were then just ripe; and I found, to my surprise, that my female cousins were quite as expert at climbing trees as the boys. I began to feel deficient in accomplishments; but I was not sufficiently a hoyden to follow their example, and could only perform the part of an admiring spectator.

A very quiet-looking old horse was grazing near by, and my cousins proposed that we should have a ride. I surveyed the great tall animal with dismay, and was frightened at the idea of being perched on his back; but the boys lifted me up, and five of us were soon mounted, ready for a start. It was our intention to proceed in this triumphant manner to the woods to gather berries; but our proposed conductor evidently disapproved the projected excursion, for, with a sudden kick-up behind, he sent us all five rolling on the grass. My white frock was the sufferer as usual; and scarcely any evil that has befallen me since, ever affected me more than would the dreaded spot that always appeared in the most conspicuous place whenever I was dressed up. It was always the herald of speedy disgrace, either in the shape of being sent supperless to bed, or deprived of going out next day. Mammy was particularly severe on such occasions; it was provoking to be sure, after taking the pains to dress me nicely, to find all her work spoiled within the next fifteen minutes; but I did think it was not my fault, and wondered how it always happened. My new companions could not understand my distress in consequence of this accident; and with trembling steps I went in to Aunt Henshaw, expecting to be kept by her side for the rest of the day, and never brought out again.

What was my surprise when, after examining the spot, she

said, in a tone which sounded like music in my ears: "Well child, you couldn't help it, and it is well you were not hurt. After all, white dresses are poor things for children to play in, and this is only fit for the wash-tub now. But this is not quite so bad as the pig-pen—eh, Amy?"

The color mounted quickly into my face at these last words, and gladly obeying her injunction to "go, play now," I bounded from the room; while Aunt Henshaw, I suppose, enlightened the company as to the meaning of her question, and my evident confusion. Oh, if people did but know the effect of kind words, especially when harshness is expected! I never enjoyed romping so much in all my life as on that afternoon; Aunt Henshaw had pronounced my dress "fit only for the wash-tub," and I thought that before it proceeded thither, it might just as well be a little more soiled as not. So we rolled about on the grass, climbed over fences, and rambled through the woods without fear or restraint. With a light and happy heart I set out on the journey home, congratulating myself that I was not then to encounter the eagle eyes of Mammy.

Aunt Henshaw, though perfectly willing that I should enjoy myself at play, did not approve of my spending my whole time in idleness; and under her superintendence, I felt more disposed to work than I ever had before. With her assistance I completed several articles of dress for a sister of Sylvia's, who was very poor, and lived in a sort of hovel near by; and the indefatigable Holly having again discovered the kittens in some equally out-of-the-way place, I at last, with a great deal of difficulty, succeeded in manufacturing a warm suit of clothes for the winter wear of the prettiest one. Having equipped the kitten in its new habiliments, I carried it to Aunt Henshaw, as quite a triumph of art; but when I made my appearance, with the two little ears poking out of the bonnet, and the tail quite visible through a hole in the skirt which I had cut for it, Cousin Statia actually indulged in a hearty fit of laughter, while Aunt Henshaw appeared even more amused. She told me that nature had furnished it with a covering quite sufficient to protect it from the cold; but I thought that it must then be a great deal too warm in summer, and had just commenced fanning it, when she explained to me that the fur was a great deal thinner in summer than in winter. This satisfied me; and releasing the astonished kitten from its numerous wrappers, I presented them to Holly, and gave up all idea of furnishing it with a wardrobe.

CHAPTER XIII

At Aunt Henshaw's, my passion for rummaging drawers and boxes of knickknacks was abundantly gratified. The old lady fairly over-flowed with the milk of human kindness, and allowed me to put her things in disorder as often as I chose. There was an album quilt, among her possessions, which I never grew tired of admiring. The pieces were all of an octagon shape, arranged in little circles of different colors; and in the centre of each circle was a piece of white muslin, on which was written in tiny characters the name of the person who had made the circle, and two lines of poetry. This album quilt was a good many years old; and had been made by the ladies of the neighborhood, as a tribute of respect to Aunt Henshaw, on account of her many acts of bravery and presence of mind during the trying times of the Revolution.

The old lady was never weary of describing the grand quilting, which took place in an old stone barn on the premises; when they all came at one o'clock, and sitting down to work, scarcely spoke a word until six, when the quilt was triumphantly pronounced to be completed; and taking it from the frame, they proceeded to arrange a large table, set out with strawberries and cream, dough-nuts, chickens, cider, and almost every incongruous eatable that could be mentioned. Washington was then President, and after drinking his health in cider, coffee, and tea, which last was then a very precious commodity, being served in cups exactly the size of a doll's set, they all in turn related stories or personal anecdotes of the great General, of whom Aunt Henshaw never spoke without the greatest reverence and enthusiasm. He died when I was very young, so that I never saw him; but I have visited his tomb, and his residence at Mount Vernon, and have also seen portraits of him that were pronounced to be life-like by those who were intimately acquainted with him.

Aunt Henshaw had actually entertained La Fayette at her house for a whole night, and she showed me the very room he slept in; while Cousin Statia produced an album in which he had written his name. I always experienced a burning desire to possess some memento of the distinguished men whose names are woven in the annals of our country; and seating myself at the table with the album before me, I spent several hours in trying to copy the illustrious autograph. But all my efforts were vain; I could produce nothing like it, and was obliged to return the book to its favored owner.

I delighted to spell out the album quilt until I knew almost every line by heart; while the curious medley which these different scraps of poetry presented reminded me very much of a play, in which one person repeats a line, to which another must find a rhyme. When Aunt Henshaw died, which was just about the time that I was grown up, she left the quilt to me in her will; because, as she said. I had always been so fond of it. I still have it carefully packed away, and regard it as quite a treasure.

But very often, during a voyage of discoveries through rooms that were seldom used, I passed various boxes, and awkward-looking little trunks, and curious baskets, that struck me as being particularly interesting in appearance. But Aunt Henshaw always said: "Those are Statia's—we must not touch them," and passed quickly on, without in the least

Ella Rodman

indulging my excited curiosity. Whether Cousin Statia kept wild animals, or mysterious treasures, or old clothes, in all these places, I was unable to conclude; but I determined to find out if possible. Having one day accompanied her upstairs, she proceeded to unlock a large trunk which I had always regarded with longing eyes; and opening them very wide, that I might take in as much as possible in a hasty survey, what was my disappointment to see her take out a couple of linen pillow-cases, nicely ruffled, while at least a dozen or two more remained, together with a corresponding number of sheets, table-cloths, napkins, &c.! All of home-made manufacture, and seeming to my youthful ideas enough to last a life-time. What could Cousin Statia possibly do with all these things? Or what had she put them there for? I knew that Aunt Henshaw possessed inexhaustible stores, and I could not imagine why Cousin Statia found it necessary to have her's separate. I pondered the matter over for two or three days, and then concluded to apply to Holly for information on the desired point.

"Why, lor bless you!" said the colored girl in a mysterious manner, "Didn't you know that Miss Statia has been crossed in love?"

Holly announced this fact as a sufficiently explanatory one; but I could not comprehend what connection there was between being crossed in love, and a large trunk of bran new things.

"Why, I quite pities your ignorance, Miss Amy! In old times," continued my informant, as though dwelling on her own particular virtue in this respect, "in old times people didn't used to be half so lazy as they am now-a-days, and thought nothing at all of sewing their fingers to the bone, or spinning their nails off, or knittin' forever; and when gals growed up, and had any thoughts of gittin' married, they set to work and made hull trunks full of things, and people used to call them spinsters. Now Miss Statia has been fillin' trunks and baskets ever sense she could do anything, so that she's got a pretty likely stock—but no one ever came along this way but what was married already, and that's the meanin' of bein' crossed in love. But don't for your life go to tellin' nobody—they'd most chop my head off, if it should come out."

I asked Holly how she had ascertained the fact; "Oh," she replied, knowingly, "there ain't much that escapes me. I know pretty much every article in this house, and hear whatever's goin' on. Key-holes is a great convenience; and though it ain't very pleasant to be squatin' in cold entries, and fallin' in the room sometimes, when people open the door without no warnin', yet I'm often there when they think I'm safe in the kitchin. Miss Statia once boxed my ears and sent me to bed, when she happened to ketch me listinin'; but it didn't smart much, and people can't 'spect to gather roses without thistles."

Holly often interspersed her conversation with various quotations and wise reflections; but the idea of listening at key-holes quite shocked my sense of honor, and I endeavored to remonstrate with her upon the practice.

"It won't do for you to talk so, Miss Amy," was her sagacious reply; "you mus'n't quarrel with the ship that carries you safe over. If I had not listened at key-holes, you'd never have known what was in them trunks."

The truth of this remark was quite manifest; and concluding that I was not exactly suited to the character of admonisher, I never renewed the attempt.

Aunt Henshaw had boxes of old letters which she estimated among her greatest valuables; and sometimes, when the sun was shining brightly without, and the soft air of summer

Ella Rodman

waving the trees gently to and fro, the old lady would invite me in a mysterious manner to her room, and drawing forth an almost endless package, open letter after letter, and read to me the correspondence of people whom I cared nothing about. I tried very hard to suppress all signs of yawning, for I wanted to be out at play; but I must have been ungrateful not to exercise a little patience with one so kind and affectionate, and she, dear old soul! evidently considered it the greatest treat she could offer me. I became in this manner acquainted with the whole history of her courtship; and charmed with so quiet a listener, she would read to me till I fairly fell asleep. But her thoughts being entirely occupied with the past, and her eyes in endeavoring to decipher the faded hand-writing, this inattention passed unobserved; and she pursued her reading until called off by her daily duties.

Dear old lady! how often have I watched her when she was asleep, as with the neat white frill of her cap partially shading her face, she sat in the large chair with her hands folded together, and her spectacles lying on the book in her lap. She looked so pure and calm that I sometimes felt afraid that she might be dead, like old people I had heard of who died quietly in their sleep; but I could not bear the idea, and a feeling of inexpressible relief would come over me when I beheld the lids slowly rise again from the mild eyes that were ever bent lovingly upon me.

She bad a box piled with rolls of manuscript containing poetry, which she told me she had taken great pleasure in composing. "Saturday nights," said she, "when everything was in order, and, the next day being Sunday, I had no household cares to think of, I would amuse myself in composing verses that were seldom shown to any one. Mr. Henshaw was a most excellent man and a kind husband, but he had no taste for poetry, and considered it a great waste of time. Another thing that helped to set him against it was an unfortunate poem that I composed on the event of a marriage that took place in the neighborhood. The gentleman had courted the lady for a number of years without success; and after praising his constancy, I dwelt on the beauteous Eliza's charms, and said something about winning the goal at last. But they were very much offended; they supposed that I was ridiculing them, and said that I had represented them as doing a great many foolish things which they had never thought of. There was no use in attempting to pacify them—I had thrown away my poetry where it was not appreciated; and Mr. Henshaw exclaimed in a tone of annoyance: 'Now do, I beg of you, never let me see you again at the writing-desk! You have done as much mischief with your pen as other women accomplish with their tongues.' So I never sent poetry again to other people; but whenever I felt lonely, I sat down and wrote, and it has really been a great comfort to me. One of these days, Amy, I shall give this all to you."

When I returned home, the poetry was carefully laid in the bottom of my trunk; but I have my suspicions that for sometime after Jane kindled the nursery fire with it. While looking over her things one day. Aunt Henshaw showed me an old-fashioned pair of ear-rings, which I admired very much.

"I intended to give these to you, Amy," said she, "but I see that your ears have not been pierced."

"Why, I thought those holes always grew in people's ears!" said I, in surprise. "Have I none in mine?"

"No," she replied, "they are always made with a needle, or some sharp instrument."

"Does it hurt?" I inquired.

"Not much," was her reply, and so the subject dropped, but I still pursued it in thought.

Ella Rodman

I fancied myself decked with the ear-rings, and the pleasure I should experience in showing them to Mammy and Jane; but then on the other hand, the idea of the needle was anything but agreeable, for I could not bear the least pain. I wavered for sometime between the advantages and disadvantages of the operation. This state of mind led me to notice people's ears much more than I had formerly done; and perceiving that Sylvia's were adorned with a pair of large gold hoops, I applied to her for advice.

"Why, Miss Amy!" she exclaimed, in surprise, "you are real shaller, if you don't have your ears bored after that! Why, I'd made a hole in my nose in half a minit, if somebody'd only give me a gold ring to put through it!"

"Who bored *your* ears, Sylvia?" said I at length.

"Why, I did it myself, to be sure. Any body can do that—jest take a needle and thread and draw it right through."

I shuddered involuntarily; but just then Sylvia moved her head a little, and the rings shook and glittered so fascinatingly that I resolved to become a martyr to the cause of vanity. The colored woman having agreed to perform the office, and Aunt Henshaw and Statia being out for the afternoon, I seated myself on a chair with my back against the dresser; while Sylvia mounted the few steps that led to her sleeping-room in order to search for a needle, and Holly endeavored to keep up my courage by representing the fascinating appearance I should present when decorated with ear-rings.

Sylvia soon came down, with needle, and thread, and cork; while I began to tremble and turn pale on perceiving the instruments of torture. I had quite forgotten how disagreeable needles felt in the flesh; and Sylvia's first attempt was brought to a sudden end by a loud scream, which would certainly have roused the neighbors had there been any near.

"Now, Miss Amy!" she exclaimed, "I had your ear almost bored then. But if you're going to cut up such didos I shall leave off directly—it ain't no such great fun for me."

She was going up stairs with a very resolute air, and again the ear-rings flashed and glittered; and having by this time lost the acute sense of pain, I called her back and begged her to proceed.

"Now mind," said she, "if you holler again, I'll jest stop at once."

I glued my lips firmly together, while she again adjusted the cork and needle; but I could hardly bear it, and trembled like an aspen leaf. One ear was soon pierced, while I felt the needle in every part of my frame; and Sylvia was proceeding to do the other, but I jumped up suddenly, exclaiming: "Oh Sylvia! I cannot have the other one bored! It will kill me!"

"Well, I wouldn't if I was you, Miss Amy," said she, "cos you can hang both rings in one ear, you know—and that'll look real beautiful, won't it, Holly?"

Holly burst into a loud fit of laughter, and through the effects of ridicule, I submitted a second time to the infliction. But it was impossible to endure the suffering any longer; the color gradually faded from my face, and just as Sylvia concluded, she found that I had fainted. The two were very much frightened, and after almost drowning me with water, they lifted me up and carried me to my own bed. Aunt Henshaw soon came home, and her horror at my situation was only equalled by her astonishment. Sylvia did not tell her the cause of my sudden illness; but she soon discovered it by a glance at my ears which were much inflamed and swollen, having been pierced in a very bungling manner. Sylvia

Ella Rodman

received such a severe reprimand that she was almost angry enough to leave on the spot; but she had only erred through ignorance, and I succeeded at length in reconciling her mistress.

"But, my dear Amy," said the kind old lady, as she sat down beside me, "Why is it that you are always getting into some trouble if left to yourself for ever so short a time? You cannot tell the pain it gives me. Why, an account of your various scrapes since you have been here would almost fill a book."

What could I reply? It was a natural and most unfortunate propensity which displayed itself everywhere; as well with Mammy in the precincts of the nursery, as when roaming about at Aunt Henshaw's.

"But the ear-rings?" said I. "You will give them to me now, will you not? I should *so* much like to have them!"

"And so you shall have them, dear," replied Aunt Henshaw. "It would he cruel to refuse them after your suffering so much for them. But I never would have mentioned them had I had any idea of such an unfortunate result."

Supposing that it would please me, she got them out of the case and laid them beside me. They were very pretty, to be sure, but oh! how much suffering those ear-rings caused me! My poor ears were very sore for a long time, and I would sit for hours leaning my head on a pillow, in hopes of easing the pain. And yet, when they were at last well, and the ear-rings really in, I almost forgot what I had suffered in the delight I experienced at my supposed transformation. They were the admiration of the kitchen; and even Aunt Henshaw and Cousin Statia allowed that ear-rings were a great improvement; and I began to think that on my return home they would even throw Ellen Tracy's curls into the shade.

The summer was passing away—harvest had come and gone; and while the others were engaged during this busy season, I was to be seen perched on every load of hay, from which I had of course two or three tumbles, but always on some pile beneath. The kittens had grown large and awkward, and consequently lost my favor; while the cat no longer put herself to the trouble of hiding them, so that I could now have them whenever I chose—coming like most other privileges when no longer desired. The evenings were getting chilly, so that a fire was very acceptable; and I loved to sit by the bright flame before the candles were brought in, and listen to Aunt Henshaw's stories.

"Now," said I one evening when we had all comfortably arranged ourselves to spend the twilight in doing nothing, "do tell me a very interesting story, Aunt Henshaw—for you know that I am going home soon, and perhaps it is the last that I shall hear."

"Well," said she with a smile, "if it is to be so very interesting, I must think very hard first."

Cousin Statia had been looking towards the door, when she suddenly inquired: "Did you ever tell her about the bullet hole?"

"Why, no," replied the old lady, "I do not believe I ever did. Have you noticed the round hole in the front door, Amy?"

I replied in the negative; and taking me into the hall, she led the way to the front door which opened in two parts, and in the upper half I distinctly perceived a bullet hole which had been made by the British; and it was the story attached to this very hole which she was about to tell me.

"Well, one night," said she, "a long while ago, I sat by the fire with the baby in my arms, while the other children were

Ella Rodman

playing around. The two women servants were in the kitchen, and Mr. Henshaw had taken the men several miles off, on some business relating to the farm. It was just about this time, before the candles were lit; and one of the women came in to tell me that five British soldiers were approaching the house.

"Fasten all the doors then," said I, "and let no one enter unless I give you permission."

The doors were well fastened up, and before long I heard them knocking with the ends of their muskets. I let them knock for some time; but at length I raised an upper window, and asked them what they wanted.

"We want some supper," they replied, "and will probably stay all night."

"It is not in my power to accommodate you." I replied, as coolly as possible, "nor do I feel willing to admit any visitors in the absence of my husband."

"If you do not admit us soon we will break the door down!" they exclaimed.

"Of that I am not much afraid," said I; "it is too well secured."

I withdrew from the window, and for half an hour they tried various means of effecting an entrance, but it was impossible. I approached the window again, and they called out: "If you do not have the door opened, we shall certainly fire!"

"Do so," I replied; "there is no one to injure by it except helpless women and children."

I did not suppose they would do it—I thought it was intended only for a threat; and was therefore as much surprised as any of the others, when a bullet came whizzing through the front door, and passing through a pane of glass in an opposite window, fell into the yard. A dreadful scream arose from the servants, and perhaps frightened for the effects, or perceiving my husband and the men, they made a hasty retreat; and I was just ready to sink from fright when Mr. Henshaw came in. He told me never to stop up the bullet-hole, but to leave it to show what women were made of in the Revolution.

Ella Rodman

CHAPTER XIV

Cousin Statia had completed her winter's knitting, Aunt Henshaw began to make pumpkin pies, and the period of my visit was rapidly drawing to a close. The letters from home grew more and more solicitous for my return, and at last the day was fixed. I felt anxious to see them all again, and yet rather sorry to lay aside my present state of freedom. I had quite escaped from leading-strings, and found it very pleasant to follow the bent of my inclination as I had done at Aunt Henshaw's; but absence had banished all memory of the thorns I had sometimes encountered in my career at home, and I thought only of the roses—the idea of change being also a great inducement.

Holly and I had passed whole afternoons in gathering hazelnuts which grew near a fence not far from the house; and having filled a very respectable-sized bag with them, I felt quite impatient at the idea of returning home well-laden with supplies, like any prudent housekeeper. Aunt Henshaw was to accompany me, and selecting some of her choicest produce, and an immense bunch of herbs, as antidotes for all the aches and ills which human flesh is heir to, on a bright, glowing September morning, we set forward on my homeward journey. "Blessings brighten as they leave us;" and although I had been considered the torment of the whole household, all regretted my departure, and begged me to come soon again.

"Now, Miss Amy," said Sylvia, as I was taking a long private farewell in the kitchen, "jest take a piece of advice from an old colored woman what has lived longer in the world than you have, and roasted chickens and fried sassages ever sense she can remember. Buckwheat cakes is very good, but to keep your own counsel is a heap better—so when you go home don't you go to telling about that ere pig-pen business, or the time when the old hen flewed at you, or tumbling off the old horse. People that don't say nothin' often gits credit for bein' quite sensible, and p'raps you can deceive 'em too; for you'll be kind o' made a fuss with when you fust get home, and if you don't let on about all these here scrapes they'll think more of you."

Sylvia's advice struck me as being very sensible, and I therefore resolved to act upon it, and endeavor to make them consider me quite a different character from the hoyden Amy. I kissed Cousin Statia, who took up her sewing as calmly as though nothing of any importance was about to occur; and having delighted Holly's eyes with a bright ribbon in which all the colors of the rainbow seemed combined, I presented Sylvia with a collar worked by myself, and passed out to the stage, which was waiting for us. Our journey home was quite an uneventful one; and the wind being more favorable, we were not so long on the passage.

My parents were watching for us with anxious solicitude; but when the door opened in bounded a wild, blooming hoyden, in whose sparkling eyes and glowing cheeks they could detect no trace of the delicate invalid. Henry and Fred, with a troop of younger brothers, stood ready to devour me with kisses; but Mammy, rushing impulsively forward, pushed them all aside, and cried and laughed over me alternately, while she almost crushed me with the violence of her affection. Before I was well seated, Fred spied out the bag of hazel-nuts; and a vigorous sound of cracking informed me that the work of devastation had already commenced.

Ella Rodman

How they all stared at my ear-rings! But mamma turned pale and burst into tears; while I stood still, feeling very uncomfortable, and yet not being exactly aware of the manner in which I had displeased her. Aunt Henshaw, however, with a minute accuracy that struck me as being painfully correct, related every circumstance connected with that unfortunate business, from her finding me extended on the bed to the time when the rings were placed in my ears.

"Oh Amy! how could you!" exclaimed my mother; "I have always despised the barbarous practice of making holes in the flesh for the sake of ornament," she continued, "but to have them pierced by an ignorant colored woman! Come here, child, and let me look at your ears. They are completely spoiled!" she exclaimed, "the holes are one-sided, and close to the very bone! What is to be done?"

Aunt Henshaw suggested that it would be better to let those grow up, and have others made in the right place; but I still retained a vivid recollection of that scene of torture, and did not therefore feel willing to have it repeated. But the earrings must come out—they were no ornament all one-sided; so they were laid away in cotton, while I had the pleasure of reflecting on the suffering I had endured for nothing. Being thus brought down at the very commencement of my attempt to be sensible, and finding it less trouble to resume my natural character, I concluded to disregard Sylvia's well-meant advice. I was very poor at keeping a secret; so one by one all the scrapes in which I had figured came to light, to the great horror of the others, and the delight of Fred, who was quite pleased to discover a congenial soul.

Mammy at length seized upon me again, and carrying me almost by force to the nursery, she locked the door and sat down beside me; determined, as she said, to have me to herself for a while. Having requested an account of all the adventures I had met with, she listened with the most absorbed attention while I unfolded the various circumstances of my visit. Mammy was sometimes amused, sometimes frightened, and often shocked, but generally for the dignity of the family; for as I had been its representative, she feared that it would suffer in the eyes of the country people.

Time passed on; Aunt Henshaw returned home, and things proceeded in their usual way. My vanity was flattered by the increased attention which I met with on all sides; my parents appeared to consider me much less of a child since my return, and I was in consequence almost emancipated from the nursery; while Mammy and Jane no longer chided me for my misdemeanors—which, to say the truth, were much less frequent than formerly.

But I soon after experienced a great source of regret in the departure of Ellen Tracy for boarding-school. Not being an only daughter like myself, her parents could better spare her; but we were almost inconsolable at parting, and having shed abundance of tears, presented each other with keepsakes as mementos of our unchanging friendship. Hers was a little china cup, which I have kept to this day, while I gave her a ring made of my own hair; so that, for want of Ellen's company, I was obliged to take up with her brother's; and the boys complained that I kept Charles so much to myself it was impossible to make him join any of their excursions.

It was my twelfth birthday; and on the evening of that day I feared that Mammy's oft-repeated threat of leaving us, at which we had so often trembled in our younger days, was about to be verified. A married sister was taken very ill, and Mammy was immediately sent for to take care of her; and indeed we were afraid that she would be obliged to stay there altogether, on account of her nephews and nieces. How dreary the nursery seemed after her departure! In vain did the good-natured Jane exert herself to tell her most amusing stories; they had lost their interest; and yielding to her

Ella Rodman

feelings, she became at length as dull as any of us.

In about a week Mammy returned; but we could see that she was changed; her sister had died and left five children but illy provided for. Through the influence of my father, different situations were obtained for the three eldest; while the old nurse, with the assistance of occasional charity, supported the two younger ones. But Mammy had suffered from sleepless nights, and rooms but illy warmed; and her own health failed during her ceaseless watch by the bedside of her sister. We did not know exactly what it was, but felt very sure that Mammy seemed no longer like the same person.

Children who are kept at a distance by their parents and elders, often have very queer thoughts, whose existence no one imagines. I do not think I was an ordinary child; and notwithstanding my hoyden nature had a very thoughtful turn of mind. I well recollect, on being once sent early to bed for some misdemeanor I bribed my brother Fred to accompany me; and waking up during the night, the saying that "he who goes to bed in anger has the devil for his bed-fellow" came across my mind, and impressed me so strongly that I caught hold of Fred's foot to ascertain whether it was so disagreeable a guest, or my own madcap brother who was lying beside me. Even the kick I received in return was rather welcome than otherwise, as it proved beyond a doubt that it was really the veritable Fred.

But what has this to do with Mammy? you ask. A great deal, I can assure you; for I began to fear that it was not the old nurse who had returned to us, but some strange being, who, having assumed her appearance, had not been able altogether to imitate her manner. So I kept myself aloof, and felt afraid to venture too close; but she grew thinner and paler, and my mother relieved her from all care of the children.

I slept in a small closet that opened into the nursery; and calling me very softly one night, she said, "Miss Amy, will you bring me a pitcher of water? I know they would not let me have it," she continued as I attempted to remonstrate with her, "but I am determined not to die choking."

I was very much frightened, but I could not see her suffer with thirst; and bringing her a large pitcher of water, she drank almost half of it at once. "Now place it on a chair where I can reach it," said she, "and go back to bed—I shall be better soon."

I did as she requested, and, childlike, soon fell asleep again. The old nurse too slept—but hers was the sleep that knows no waking. They came in the next morning and found her dead. Her features were peaceful as though she had died calmly, and beside her stood the pitcher empty. She always said that if she should ever be ill, she *would* have water—she would drink till she died, and she had literally done so. We all felt very sad, and Fred broke forth into loud screams, on being told of her death.

It was my first realization of death—the first corpse I had ever seen; and as I knelt beside the coffin, where the pale hands that lay cross-folded on the breast, the motionless features, and the dreadful stillness of the whole figure, spoke eloquently of the change that had taken place, I thought of my many acts of wilfulness, ingratitude, and unkindness, which had often pained the loving heart that had now forever ceased to beat. Could I but see those still features again animated with life, I felt that never again would my tongue utter aught but words of kindness; but it was now too late for amendment—there was nothing left me but repentance.

My parents too grieved at her death; she had been in the family so long that they were loathe to miss the old familiar face from its post in the nursery. She was buried from our own house; and there were more true mourners at her funeral than often fall to the lot of the great and gifted.

CHAPTER XV

"Papa, have you any relations?" I asked one evening rather suddenly, after pondering over the subject and wondering why it was that our family consisted of no one but papa, and mamma, and us children; while other people always had aunts, or uncles, or cousins living with them. We had plenty, to be sure, who came and made visits at different times; but I meant some one to live with us altogether.

"What a curious question!" said my father, smiling, "And how suddenly you bolted out with it, Amy, after at least half an hour's silence. You must have thought deeply on the subject, but what put it into your head just now?"

Not knowing exactly what to say, I wisely remained silent; and turning to my mother, he continued in a low tone: "Do you know that this random question of Amy's has awakened some not very welcome reminiscences, and pointed out a line of duty which does not promise much pleasure beyond the consciousness of doing right? I ought to invite an addition to the family without delay."

"Are you joking, or in earnest?" inquired my mother, "And if in earnest, pray whom do you refer to?"

"You will soon find it to be most solid, substantial earnest," rejoined my father, "for I must this very evening write a

Ella Rodman

letter to Mrs. Chesbury, senior, the step-mother of whom you have heard me speak, inviting her to spend the summer with us. She has, you know, resided at the South since my father's death, occasionally visiting her relatives at the North; and as we have never yet been honored with her company, that pleasure is still in store for us. My recollections of her, to be sure, are not so very delightful. She was very severe in her discipline, and continually checked my pleasures and enjoyments, which she usually exchanged for some long, heavy, incomprehensible task; and at the first blunder in recitation, off came her shoe, which she immediately laid across my shoulders with the most unremitting zeal. I recollect her whipping me one day when it really appeared to me that I had not been in the least to blame. I was quite a little fellow then, and drawing my hand across my eyes, I sobbed forth: 'I wish one of us in this room was dead, I do—I don't wish it was me—and I don't wish it was the cat—' Whatever I had intended to add was suddenly cut short; and I began to think that it was rather foolish of me to subject myself to two whippings instead of one. I have quite escaped from leading-strings now," added my father with an expressive look; but the old lady may be of considerable assistance in keeping you young ones in order.

The children looked frightened; and Fred, being now too old to dread any whippings on his own account, kindly undertook the instruction of his younger brothers in the art of being saucy and playing practical jokes. We were told to call her "grandmother," and treat her with the greatest respect; but as I dwelt upon my father's account of her, like the magician in olden story, I almost trembled at the visitor I had invoked. The letter was written and despatched; and after a while, an answering one received, in which the step-mother accepted her son-in-law's invitation, "for the sake," as she said, "of the many happy hours they had formerly enjoyed together." I sat reading in a distant corner of the room when this letter was received, almost concealed by the folds of the curtains; and the other children being out of the room, I overheard my father say:

"I do not remember much else but being whipped, and sent supperless to bed; if they *were* happy hours, it must have been on the principle of the frogs—'What is play to you is death to us.'"

My mother smiled; but she replied softly: "Perhaps she is changed now, Arthur; do not say anything against her before the children, for she is a stranger, entitled to our hospitality —and I would not have her welcome a chilling one."

In process of time the old lady arrived, accompanied by a colored servant who answered to the name of Venus. Fred christened her "the black divinity," at which she became highly offended; and ever after, there was a perpetual war of words waging between the two. My grandmother was a small, dark-complexioned woman, with an exceedingly haughty, and very repulsive expression. She received all her daughter-in-law's endeavors to make her feel at home as a natural right; and appeared to consider other people intended only for her sole use and benefit. As I glanced from her to my mother's fair, soft beauty, and strikingly sweet expression, I formed a comparison between the two not much to my grandmother's advantage.

We soon found that the old lady had a great idea of taking the reins into her own hands; the children were scolded, and threatened, and locked up in dark closets, until, to use their own expression, they became, most "dreadfully good," and never dared to show off under the espionage of those eagle eyes. During the summer, our parents were absent for some weeks on a pleasure jaunt; and Grandmother Chesbury having the entire control of us, we were obliged to behave very differently from usual. She kept us all in awe except Fred; but on him it was impossible to make the least impression. If she tyrannized over the rest us, it was abundantly repaid by the teazings of my mischievous brother.

The old lady was extremely violent in temper, and after irritating it to the highest pitch, or, as he termed it, "putting on the steam," he provoked her still more by his polite sarcasms and tantalizing replies. The object of contest between them was generally the last word in the argument; and when victory appeared to incline neither to one side nor the other, my grandmother would exclaim angrily: "Hold your tongue this moment, you impertinent boy! Not another word."

"Yes'm," Fred would reply, with every appearance of submission.

Having triumphed up stairs, he generally went in search of Venus, whose anger was almost as vehement as that of her mistress. Her time, when not attending to Mrs. Chesbury, was chiefly occupied by the duties of the toilet; and Jane asserted that she had anxiously inquired if there were no respectable colored gentlemen about the place? Venus always bestowed a great deal of pains on the arrangement of her head covering, which was profusely decorated with combs of various shapes and sizes; but "thereby hangs a tale" which must be told.

Good beef is very scarce at the South, and Southerners therefore consider it a great treat when they come North. My grandmother was very fond of it frizzled; and Venus being quite *au fait* in the manufacture of this dish, the old lady never allowed any one else to make it for her. One afternoon, during my parents' absence, the children being disposed of in various ways—some had gone out for a walk, two were playing together in a closet where they had been locked up, and others were rambling about the grounds—the house was pretty clear; so my grandmother resolved to enjoy a treat in her own apartment. A small table was nicely laid out with all the requisites for a comfortable tea, and Venus then departed to the kitchen to dish up some frizzled beef.

But it so happened that the odor of the savory dish, in its passage up stairs, found its way to the nostrils of Master Fred, who had been quietly engaged in some wonderfully wise researches in the library; and as even philosophers are not exempt from the earth-born love of good things, out rushed our student with a polite request that Venus would "allow him to taste the trash, and see if it was fit to be sent to Mrs. Chesbury." A scuffle ensued, in which Fred succeeded in satisfying his curiosity; and with considerably ruffled plumage, and not in the sweetest state of mind, Venus proceeded up stairs. Fred slyly followed; and peeping through the key-hole of a door that opened into my grandmother's room, he determined to watch the progress of the feast. Things looked very tempting, and he had half a mind to petition for a seat at the table; but he began to think that, even should he succeed in his request, a *seat* would be all he could gain; for the old lady attacked the eatables very much in the style of a school-boy just come home for the holidays. The frizzled beef rapidly disappeared, till the bottom of the dish was scarcely covered; but suddenly ceasing her attacks upon it, my grandmother took the dish in her hand, and pointing to some black substance, interrogated the colored girl in accents of mingled doubt and horror.

"Why Venus, come here! What—what—what *is* this?"

"Why, la, Missus!" exclaimed Venus, while every feature brightened with joyful surprise, "If there ain't my little comb, what I lost in the scuffle with Master Fred! Who would have thought to find it here!"

"Who, indeed!" ejaculated the old lady, in a voice scarcely audible.

My grandmother did not leave her room that evening, and we were told that she was ill; while it is scarcely necessary to add that Fred never again interfered with any of Venus' cookeries. When repeating the story, he always dwelt upon the ridiculous tableau presented by the horrified looks of the old lady, as she pointed to the suspicious-looking article— and the delight and surprise of Venus at recovering her lost property in such an unexpected manner. He possessed a great talent for drawing; and before long, a caricature appeared, which was a most life-like representation of the whole scene. My mother shook her head, and my father delivered a short, but expressive lecture upon the improper nature of mimicry; but in the midst of an edifying discourse Fred suddenly displayed the drawing in full view—at which all the children burst into peals of laughter, and my father abruptly closed his sermon, and frowning sternly, walked into the library; but we could perceive a nervous twitching about the corners of his mouth, which looked very much at variance with the frown upon his brow.

My mother too, fixed her eyes steadfastly upon her sewing, and refused to look up; which Fred saucily told her was only because she knew she would laugh if she did. We were then told that we had been naughty children, and sent out of the room; but somehow, we did not feel as though we had been *very* bad, or that our parents were very angry with us, and skipping along through the garden-walks, we next sent Jane almost into convulsions of laughter by a display of the picture. Mamma, however, burned it before long; she said that it was highly improper to ridicule our grandmother, even if she *had* faults, and that we must bear with her kindly, and not forget how few pleasures she enjoyed. Dear mamma! she was too kind—too good; and often met with the fate of such—imposition.

I once heard of a lady who went to a house to make a call, and stayed eleven years; this was somewhat similar to my grandmother's case—she came to pass the summer with us, and spent her life-time. Whenever she spoke of going back to the South, my father urged her to stay, and gave convincing reasons why she should prolong her visit; and my mother, too, kindly reflecting that the old lady had no near relatives and seemed to enjoy herself with us, added her entreaties. At last they told her that there was no reason why she should not stay altogether; and she appeared to think so too, for she stayed. As we grew more accustomed to her we liked her better than at first; she told us long stories about the South, and related anecdotes of the greatness, and wealth, and distinguished position of her own family, which she considered superior to any in the United States. Venus too came into more favor; and after a while we almost forgot the beef story.

Ella Rodman

CHAPTER XVI

Time passed on; I had almost reached my fifteenth birthday, and began to consider myself no longer a child. I was very tall for my age, and quite showy-looking; and gentlemen who visited at the house now treated me with all the attention due a young lady; which flattered my vanity very much, and made me think them very agreeable. I remember my father's once sending me from the room, on account of some gentleman's nonsense which he considered me too young to listen to; but I felt very much hurt at such treatment, and almost regarded myself as some heroine of romance imprisoned by cruel parents. Novels were a great injury to me, as indeed they are to every one. Their style was much more extravagant and unnatural than at the present day; and even at this early age, I had read the "Children of the Abbey," the "Mysteries of Udolpho," the "Scottish Chiefs," "Thaddeus of Warsaw," and many others of the same stamp.

But how did I obtain these, you ask? My mother, with her sense and discernment, would not have placed such books in my hands; and you are right. My grandmother was an inveterate novel-reader, but very careful that her books fell into no other hands; so that the only means of satisfying my taste for romantic reading was by stealth. Although novels were proscribed, no other books were placed in my hands; there were then scarcely any children's books published, and consumed as I was by an inordinate passion for reading, was determined to indulge it without being very particular about the means. How often have I watched my opportunity when my grandmother had left her apartment for an afternoon visit or drive, and then drawn forth the cherished volume from beneath the pillow and even from between the bed and sacking bottom! so carefully were they concealed from view. Sometimes, indeed, she locked the door of her room, and took the key with her; and then all ingress was impossible.

What wild, foolish dreams I indulged in!—What romantic-visions of the future that were never realized! How well I remember my sensations on reading the "Scottish Chiefs." Wallace appeared to me almost in the light of a god—so noble, so touching were all his acts and words, that I even envied Helen Mar the privilege of calling herself his wife, and then dying to lay her head in the same grave with him. I resolved to give up all the common-place of life, and cling unto the spiritual—to purify myself from every earth-born wish and habit, and live but in the hope of meeting with a second Wallace. I persevered in this resolution for a whole week; and then meeting with some equally delightful hero of an opposite nature, I changed from grave to gay. My mood during these periods of fascination was as variable as the different heroines I admired. Now I would imitate the pensiveness of Amanda, and go about with streaming tresses, and a softly modulated tone of voice—then I would read of some sprightly heroine who changed all by her vivacity and piquant sayings, and immediately commence springing down three stairs at a time, teazing all the children, and making some reply to everything that was said, which sometimes passed for wit but oftener for impudence—and then again some noble, self-sacrificing character would excite my admiration, and oh! how I longed for some opportunity to signalize myself! A bullet aimed at some loved one, whom I could protect by rushing forward and receiving it myself; but I was not to be killed, only sufficiently wounded to make me appear interesting—disabled in the arm, perhaps, without

Ella Rodman

much suffering, for bodily pain never formed a prominent feature in my ideas of the romantic and striking—I was too great a coward; or else a plunge into the waves to rescue some drowning person from perishing, when I wished just to come near enough to death to elevate me into a heroine for after life.

I looked in the glass, and seeing large, dark eyes, a healthful bloom, and rather pretty features, I concluded that I need not belong to the plain and amiable order, and began to wish most enthusiastically for some romantic admirer; some one who would expose himself to the danger of a sore throat and influenza for the sake of serenading me—who would be rather glad than otherwise to risk his life by jumping down a precipice to bring me some descried wild flower, and who, when away from me, would pass his time in writing extravagant poetry, of which I was to be the bright divinity. Old as I am, I feel almost ashamed to repeat this nonsense now; and had I then possessed more sense myself, or made by mother the confidant of these flights of fancy, I need not now relate my own silly experience to warn you from the effects of novel-reading.

Charles Tracy did not at all realize my romantic ideas of a hero; and one bright day the dissatisfaction which had been gradually gathering in my mind expressed itself in words. I had gone down to a lake at the bottom of the garden to indulge in high-flown meditations; and Charles Tracy stood beside one of the boats which were always kept there.

"Come, Amy," said he, as I drew near, "it is a beautiful day —let us have a row across the lake."

"No," said I, twining my arm around one of the young trees near, "I prefer remaining here."

"You had better come with me," rejoined Charles, "instead of keeping company there with the snapping-turtles. Well," he added after a short pause, "if you will not come with me, why I must go alone."

"Go, then!" said I, bitterly, "you love your own pleasure a great deal better than you do me!"

"Why Amy!" he exclaimed, coming close to me as though doubtful of my sanity, "how very strangely you talk! You know that I love you very much," he continued, "for haven't we been together and quarrelled with each other ever since I can remember? And do I not now bear the marks of the time when you threw the cat in my face to end our childish dispute? And the scar where you stuck the pen-knife in my arm? And don't you remember how you used to pull my hair out by handfuls? How can I help loving you when I call to mind all these tender recollections?"

This reply provoked me very much; and I answered energetically: "You do *not* love me!—you do not know how to love I When did you ever make any sacrifices for me?" I continued in an excited manner, "When did I ever hear you singing beneath my window in a tone meant for no ear but mine? When did you ever rush with me out of a burning house, or encounter any danger for my sake? When did you ever watch for a glimpse of my taper at midnight when all others were asleep?"

During the progress of this singular speech, Charles Tracy's countenance had gradually changed from the surprised to the amused; and when I had concluded he laughed—yes, he actually laughed! What a damper of sentiment!

"Laugh on," said I, in a dignified manner, as I turned my steps homeward, "that has now put an end to all."

He was but a boy—I, a *woman*, for should I not be fifteen

to-morrow? and I walked away from him in contempt; while he quietly jumped into the boat and rowed across the lake, whistling a tune. But I had not proceeded far before a loud "ha! ha!" from my brother Fred sounded close at my side; he had been an unobserved listener to the whole conversation, now enjoyed the pleasure of teasing me all the way home.

"That's right, Amy!" said he, "Keep up your dignity, child. What a rich scene! *'When did you ever watch for a glimpse of my taper at midnight when all others were asleep?'* Rather a hopeless watch, I'm thinking, as you sleep in the middle room between mother's and the nursery; and between you and I, Amy, you know that you don't burn a taper, but a brass lamp; but that, of course, isn't quite so poetical to tell of. Such an air, too!—what a rare tragic actress you'd make! Do say it over, won't you? I have almost forgotten the beginning."

I gave Fred a boxed ear, which must have stung for some-time afterwards; and running hastily into the house, locked myself up in my own room till tea-time. The next day was my birthday; and while my table was strewn with acceptable gifts from all the others, I perceived among them a very antiquated-looking cap and pair of spectacles, to the latter of which was attached a slip of paper, on which was written: "To improve the impaired sight of my dear sister Amy, produced by her declining years; also a cap to conceal the gray hairs of age, and 'Young's Night Thoughts' for the edification of her mind."

I was almost ready to cry from mortification; but I remem-bered that I was now fifteen, and took the articles down stairs for the purpose of exposing Master Fred, but what did I get for my pains? In justification he told the story of yesterday, in his own peculiarly humorous way; and when I saw myself thus reflected, the ridiculous tendency of my words and manner struck me forcibly, and I was almost ready to laugh. But the others did that abundantly for me, while wondering where I had picked up such notions; and Grandmother Chesbury, I verily believe, suspected that I had been at her novels, for after that I never could find one.

But although I was thus debarred from receiving any new impressions, the old ones still continued in full force; and at last came the long desired opportunity to signalize myself. I was then almost sixteen, and the treaty of peace with England had just been celebrated. I remember well the illuminations and festivities on the first night of the proclamation, which we spent in the city at a friend's house; the balconies were wreathed with flowers, lights blazed from every window, crowds of beautifully-dressed women filled the rooms, and the sounds of music and dancing were heard in every street. It was my first evening in company—my first experience of admiration; and completely carried away by the music, the lights, and the occasion, the old desire for some signalizing deed came thronging back in full force, till I grew almost bewildered. No opportunity offered that night; I could only join in the festivities, and listen to the feats and praises of others; but towards the latter part of the evening my eye was attracted by the brilliant uniform and handsome appearance of a young officer who passed through the rooms, and lingered a moment in a distant corner among a knot of friends who crowded eagerly about him. His comm.-anding figure, beautiful features, and intellectual, yet sweet, expression, completely realized all my ideas of a novel-hero; I saw my father speaking to him, and immediately made signs to introduce him, but before I could catch his eye, the officer had disappeared. Papa told me that Major Arlington's father had been an old friend of his, and he would have introduced him to me, but business called him in another direction, and he could not stay a moment longer, but promised us a visit at an early day.

You need not smile, Miss Ella, and look so knowing at the

mention of the name; how do you know that there were not two Arlingtons in the world? How do you know but that it was his brother I married? How do you know—but never mind, I will go on with my story. It was several days after that eventful evening, which still left a vivid impression upon my mind; the desire to perform some wonderful deed remained in full force, mingled with visions of the young officer, and I wandered about, without paying much attention to my ordinary duties. Papa and mamma were both from home, and Grandmother Chesbury had locked herself up with a new novel; while I was roaming about the grounds not far from the front entrance.

A sound of wheels suddenly struck upon my ear; I supposed it was some visitor and paid not much attention to it; but before long there was a confused noise of voices—a sound of plunging and rearing—and a distinct crashing of some heavy vehicle. My evil genius led me to the spot; I beheld a handsome carriage, which the horses seemed striving to dash in pieces—caught a glimpse of a glittering uniform inside—and following a wild impulse, sprang forward and endeavored to seize the bridle. I heard some one say, "Take care of the young lady!" and then the officer jumped from the carriage, while I was thrown down close to the horses' feet. A confused hum sounded in my ears—and then followed a long blank.

*   *   *   *   *

When I awoke to consciousness I found myself lying on a sofa in a small sitting-room; but no one was bending tenderly over me—not even a mother's face met my eyes—but the gossip of two women servants grated painfully on my ear.

"What under the sun possessed Miss Amy to go and cut up such a caper as that!" said one of them, "All the mischief she's done this day won't be done away with for weeks to come."

"No, indeed!" rejoined the other, "that young officer is a fixture here for six weeks at least. Rome wasn't built in a day, nor are broken legs healed in ten minutes—and such a beauty as he is, too! It's shameful to think of!"

"If she'd only let him alone, he'd done well enough—but she must go and jump right under the horses' feet, so that, of course, he had to spring out to prevent her being killed, and that broke his leg, while she wasn't hurt a bit. Speaking of beauties, if Miss Amy could only have seen herself then!— spotted with mud from head to foot, and her hair flying in all directions!"

On hearing that I was not hurt, I sprang from the sofa and rushed to the glass, where I encountered the reflection of a most pitiable-looking figure. Even my face was daubed with mud and dirt, and I looked like a veritable fright. Shame, mortification, and sorrow for my heedless conduct almost overwhelmed me. In the selfish desire to signalize myself, I had hazarded the life of a fellow-being, and brought upon him weeks of suffering which no act of mine could now alleviate. The tears rolled down my cheeks; but having ascertained that my parents had not yet returned, I cut short the gossip of the servants, and ordering them to bring me some water, I arranged my disordered dress for a visit to the sufferer's apartment.

Doctor Irwin had been instantly sent for; and when I entered the room, he was seated by his patient's bedside, while Major Arlington lay with closed eyes and pallid features in a kind of sleep or stupor.

"Miss Amy," whispered the doctor, "this is a sad business— and your parents from home, too. What will be their feelings on their return?"

I glanced at the motionless figure of the young officer, and too much ashamed to reply, hung my head in silence.

"Are you sure that you were not at all hurt, my dear child?" he continued in a kind tone; "What a very wild proceeding it was to throw yourself into the melee! If two men could not manage the horses, could you suppose that your strength would be sufficient. You should have reasoned with yourself before taking such a step, for you see the unfortunate effects of it."

Reason! there was not the least particle of reason in my whole composition; this was a wild, impulsive act, performed without the least thought for the probable conesquences, and I now stood gazing on the wreck I had made, in silent bewilderment. My parents soon returned; and hurrying to the apartment with countenances of astonishment and fear, there realized a confirmation of the dreadful accounts they had been assailed with. "And who was the author of all this mischief? *Amy.*" My eyes drooped under the stern, reproving glances I encountered, and I crept about the house like a guilty thing—fervently wishing for the bodily suffering I had brought upon the victim of my wild attempt, instead of the pain of mind with which I was tormented.

Days passed on, but the lapse of time was unheeded by me; my post was by the bedside of the sufferer—my employment to anticipate his slightest wish, and yield to every humor. As he grew better I read to him, sung to him, talked to him; and in return received the grateful glances of those expressive eyes, which followed me about whenever I moved from his side. At length he could sit up in his apartment, and then walk slowly through the grounds, with the assistance of a heavy cane on one side and my arm on the other; till at last he was pronounced to be as well as other people; or, as Dr. Irwin expressed it, "as good as new." Your eyes are brightening up, Ella, in anticipation of a most sentimental love-tale; but I shall not gratify your desire of laughing at your grandmother's folly; but shall only say, that before he left, I had promised, with the consent of my parents, to become Mrs. Arlington. I was married at eighteen, and, strange to say, to one who appeared a realization of all my girlish fancies; he was noble-minded, warm-hearted, and almost as enthusiastic as myself—with a sweetness of temper which I have never seen raffled, except by some act of injustice or cruelty.

But do not flatter yourself, Ella, that life glided on with me like the pages of a romance; I was obliged to lay aside a great many silly theories which I had indulged in, and come to plain reality much oftener than suited my inclination. A *perfect* person is not to be found upon earth; when disposed to murmur at not meeting with the sacrifices you expect, ask yourself if you would be willing to make these sacrifices for another—and then be not surprised that others are not more free from the dross of self-consideration than you are. Also, do not suppose that it was my hair-brained performance at our first meeting which attracted my husband's affections; no, often has the color mounted to my face at his reference to that scene, and his own impressions then.

"You reminded me, Amy," he would say, laughing, "of some reckless sprite from the kingdom of misrule, who had flown into the scene, determined to make all the trouble she could. It was very chivalrous of you, to be sure, and I ought to be very grateful—but I must own that I felt exceedingly provoked at being obliged to risk my life by springing out to rescue you from the horses' hoofs. But never mind, *chere amie*" he would add as he saw the hot tears starting to my eyes, while face, neck, and brow, were suffused with the hue of mortification, "there was an after-page in the sick-room, when I beheld, with surprise, my crazy heroine transformed into the demure, and gentle nurse, and learned to distinguish a soft-toned voice, which always lingered in my ears like pleasant music; so that after all, I am really indebted to you, Amy, for making me break my leg—for, if you had not done so, I am afraid I never should have discovered my jewel of a wife."

So much for my romance; but the scene generally ended with the kiss of reconciliation, and I, too, learned to smile at my act of girlish folly.

"My tale is told; my parents have long slept beside each other, where the long grass waves over them—my elder brothers are still living—my brother Henry is a beloved and venerated clergyman in one of our large cities—while the wild, hair-brained Fred became a talented lawyer in the same place where he is universally respected. The rest of my brothers are all dead; and we three only survive out of a family of nine. Perhaps at some future time I may give you an account of my residence in England; but I must now conclude my adventures for the present."

Here ended my grandmother's history, which had afforded us many evenings of amusement. We were both surprised and pleased at her frankness in speaking of her faults and mischievous acts; and could indeed hardly comprehend that the very sensible, dignified lady before us had ever been such an odd, harum-scarum sort of character—yet so it was, and she had kindly related her own experience for our improvement. The last chapter was intended more especially for my own particular edification; but we all laughed heartily at my grandmother's ideas of signalizing herself. That room is to us a charmed spot; and we look forward most anxiously to the time when she is to begin an account of her life in England.

Choose from Thousands of 1stWorldLibrary Classics By

A. M. Barnard	Booth Tarkington	Edward Everett Hale
Ada Leverson	Boyd Cable	Edward J. O'Biren
Adolphus William Ward	Bram Stoker	Edward S. Ellis
Aesop	C. Collodi	Edwin L. Arnold
Agatha Christie	C. E. Orr	Eleanor Atkins
Alexander Aaronsohn	C. M. Ingleby	Eleanor Hallowell Abbott
Alexander Kielland	Carolyn Wells	Eliot Gregory
Alexandre Dumas	Catherine Parr Traill	Elizabeth Gaskell
Alfred Gatty	Charles A. Eastman	Elizabeth McCracken
Alfred Ollivant	Charles Amory Beach	Elizabeth Von Arnim
Alice Duer Miller	Charles Dickens	Ellem Key
Alice Turner Curtis	Charles Dudley Warner	Emerson Hough
Alice Dunbar	Charles Farrar Browne	Emilie F. Carlen
Allen Chapman	Charles Ives	Emily Bronte
Alleyne Ireland	Charles Kingsley	Emily Dickinson
Ambrose Bierce	Charles Klein	Enid Bagnold
Amelia E. Barr	Charles Hanson Towne	Enilor Macartney Lane
Amory H. Bradford	Charles Lathrop Pack	Erasmus W. Jones
Andrew Lang	Charles Romyn Dake	Ernie Howard Pie
Andrew McFarland Davis	Charles Whibley	Ethel May Dell
Andy Adams	Charles Willing Beale	Ethel Turner
Angela Brazil	Charlotte M. Braeme	Ethel Watts Mumford
Anna Alice Chapin	Charlotte M. Yonge	Eugene Sue
Anna Sewell	Charlotte Perkins Stetson	Eugenie Foa
Annie Besant	Clair W. Hayes	Eugene Wood
Annie Hamilton Donnell	Clarence Day Jr.	Eustace Hale Ball
Annie Payson Call	Clarence E. Mulford	Evelyn Everett-green
Annie Roe Carr	Clemence Housman	Everard Cotes
Annonaymous	Confucius	F. H. Cheley
Anton Chekhov	Coningsby Dawson	F. J. Cross
Archibald Lee Fletcher	Cornelis DeWitt Wilcox	F. Marion Crawford
Arnold Bennett	Cyril Burleigh	Fannie E. Newberry
Arthur C. Benson	D. H. Lawrence	Federick Austin Ogg
Arthur Conan Doyle	Daniel Defoe	Ferdinand Ossendowski
Arthur M. Winfield	David Garnett	Fergus Hume
Arthur Ransome	Dinah Craik	Florence A. Kilpatrick
Arthur Schnitzler	Don Carlos Janes	Fremont B. Deering
Arthur Train	Donald Keyhoe	Francis Bacon
Atticus	Dorothy Kilner	Francis Darwin
B.H. Baden-Powell	Dougan Clark	Frances Hodgson Burnett
B. M. Bower	Douglas Fairbanks	Frances Parkinson Keyes
B. C. Chatterjee	E. Nesbit	Frank Gee Patchin
Baroness Emmuska Orczy	E. P. Roe	Frank Harris
Baroness Orczy	E. Phillips Oppenheim	Frank Jewett Mather
Basil King	E. S. Brooks	Frank L. Packard
Bayard Taylor	Earl Barnes	Frank V. Webster
Ben Macomber	Edgar Rice Burroughs	Frederic Stewart Isham
Bertha Muzzy Bower	Edith Van Dyne	Frederick Trevor Hill
Bjornstjerne Bjornson	Edith Wharton	Frederick Winslow Taylor

Friedrich Kerst
Friedrich Nietzsche
Fyodor Dostoyevsky
G.A. Henty
G.K. Chesterton
Gabrielle E. Jackson
Garrett P. Serviss
Gaston Leroux
George A. Warren
George Ade
Geroge Bernard Shaw
George Cary Eggleston
George Durston
George Ebers
George Eliot
George Gissing
George MacDonald
George Meredith
George Orwell
George Sylvester Viereck
George Tucker
George W. Cable
George Wharton James
Gertrude Atherton
Gordon Casserly
Grace E. King
Grace Gallatin
Grace Greenwood
Grant Allen
Guillermo A. Sherwell
Gulielma Zollinger
Gustav Flaubert
H. A. Cody
H. B. Irving
H. C. Bailey
H. G. Wells
H. H. Munro
H. Irving Hancock
H. R. Naylor
H. Rider Haggard
H. W. C. Davis
Haldeman Julius
Hall Caine
Hamilton Wright Mabie
Hans Christian Andersen
Harold Avery
Harold McGrath
Harriet Beecher Stowe
Harry Castlemon
Harry Coghill
Harry Houidini

Hayden Carruth
Helent Hunt Jackson
Helen Nicolay
Hendrik Conscience
Hendy David Thoreau
Henri Barbusse
Henrik Ibsen
Henry Adams
Henry Ford
Henry Frost
Henry James
Henry Jones Ford
Henry Seton Merriman
Henry W Longfellow
Herbert A. Giles
Herbert Carter
Herbert N. Casson
Herman Hesse
Hildegard G. Frey
Homer
Honore De Balzac
Horace B. Day
Horace Walpole
Horatio Alger Jr.
Howard Pyle
Howard R. Garis
Hugh Lofting
Hugh Walpole
Humphry Ward
Ian Maclaren
Inez Haynes Gillmore
Irving Bacheller
Isabel Cecilia Williams
Isabel Hornibrook
Israel Abrahams
Ivan Turgenev
J. G.Austin
J. Henri Fabre
J. M. Barrie
J. M. Walsh
J. Macdonald Oxley
J. R. Miller
J. S. Fletcher
J. S. Knowles
J. Storer Clouston
J. W. Duffield
Jack London
Jacob Abbott
James Allen
James Andrews
James Baldwin

James Branch Cabell
James DeMille
James Joyce
James Lane Allen
James Lane Allen
James Oliver Curwood
James Oppenheim
James Otis
James R. Driscoll
Jane Abbott
Jane Austen
Jane L. Stewart
Janet Aldridge
Jens Peter Jacobsen
Jerome K. Jerome
Jessie Graham Flower
John Buchan
John Burroughs
John Cournos
John F. Kennedy
John Gay
John Glasworthy
John Habberton
John Joy Bell
John Kendrick Bangs
John Milton
John Philip Sousa
John Taintor Foote
Jonas Lauritz Idemil Lie
Jonathan Swift
Joseph A. Altsheler
Joseph Carey
Joseph Conrad
Joseph E. Badger Jr
Joseph Hergesheimer
Joseph Jacobs
Jules Vernes
Julian Hawthrone
Julie A Lippmann
Justin Huntly McCarthy
Kakuzo Okakura
Karle Wilson Baker
Kate Chopin
Kenneth Grahame
Kenneth McGaffey
Kate Langley Bosher
Kate Langley Bosher
Katherine Cecil Thurston
Katherine Stokes
L. A. Abbot
L. T. Meade

L. Frank Baum
Latta Griswold
Laura Dent Crane
Laura Lee Hope
Laurence Housman
Lawrence Beasley
Leo Tolstoy
Leonid Andreyev
Lewis Carroll
Lewis Sperry Chafer
Lilian Bell
Lloyd Osbourne
Louis Hughes
Louis Joseph Vance
Louis Tracy
Louisa May Alcott
Lucy Fitch Perkins
Lucy Maud Montgomery
Luther Benson
Lydia Miller Middleton
Lyndon Orr
M. Corvus
M. H. Adams
Margaret E. Sangster
Margret Howth
Margaret Vandercook
Margaret W. Hungerford
Margret Penrose
Maria Edgeworth
Maria Thompson Daviess
Mariano Azuela
Marion Polk Angellotti
Mark Overton
Mark Twain
Mary Austin
Mary Catherine Crowley
Mary Cole
Mary Hastings Bradley
Mary Roberts Rinehart
Mary Rowlandson
M. Wollstonecraft Shelley
Maud Lindsay
Max Beerbohm
Myra Kelly
Nathaniel Hawthrone
Nicolo Machiavelli
O. F. Walton
Oscar Wilde
Owen Johnson
P.G. Wodehouse
Paul and Mabel Thorne

Paul G. Tomlinson
Paul Severing
Percy Brebner
Percy Keese Fitzhugh
Peter B. Kyne
Plato
Quincy Allen
R. Derby Holmes
R. L. Stevenson
R. S. Ball
Rabindranath Tagore
Rahul Alvares
Ralph Bonehill
Ralph Henry Barbour
Ralph Victor
Ralph Waldo Emmerson
Rene Descartes
Ray Cummings
Rex Beach
Rex E. Beach
Richard Harding Davis
Richard Jefferies
Richard Le Gallienne
Robert Barr
Robert Frost
Robert Gordon Anderson
Robert L. Drake
Robert Lansing
Robert Lynd
Robert Michael Ballantyne
Robert W. Chambers
Rosa Nouchette Carey
Rudyard Kipling
Saint Augustine
Samuel B. Allison
Samuel Hopkins Adams
Sarah Bernhardt
Sarah C. Hallowell
Selma Lagerlof
Sherwood Anderson
Sigmund Freud
Standish O'Grady
Stanley Weyman
Stella Benson
Stella M. Francis
Stephen Crane
Stewart Edward White
Stijn Streuvels
Swami Abhedananda
Swami Parmananda
T. S. Ackland

T. S. Arthur
The Princess Der Ling
Thomas A. Janvier
Thomas A Kempis
Thomas Anderton
Thomas Bailey Aldrich
Thomas Bulfinch
Thomas De Quincey
Thomas Dixon
Thomas H. Huxley
Thomas Hardy
Thomas More
Thornton W. Burgess
U. S. Grant
Upton Sinclair
Valentine Williams
Various Authors
Vaughan Kester
Victor Appleton
Victor G. Durham
Victoria Cross
Virginia Woolf
Wadsworth Camp
Walter Camp
Walter Scott
Washington Irving
Wilbur Lawton
Wilkie Collins
Willa Cather
Willard F. Baker
William Dean Howells
William le Queux
W. Makepeace Thackeray
William W. Walter
William Shakespeare
Winston Churchill
Yei Theodora Ozaki
Yogi Ramacharaka
Young E. Allison
Zane Grey